One Love Chigusa

Soji Shimada

Known as 'Japan's Man of Mystery' and the master of postmodern whodunnits, Soji Shimada is one of Japan's most famous authors.

Shimada originally wanted to become a painter, but turned instead to reinventing the art of mystery writing. His literary debut came with his locked-room mystery *The Tokyo Zodiac Murders*, now ranked internationally as one of the best ever written. It put Shimada on the literary map overnight.

Many of Shimada's works have been adapted for film and television in Japan, and despite only a limited number of the highly-prolific Shimada's works being available in English translation, one of his books has already been ranked *Sunday Times* Best Book of the Year.

He is the recipient of the Japan Mystery Literature Award and the founder of three literary awards.

Translator: David Warren

David Warren was British Ambassador to Japan from 2008 to 2012 and Chairman of the Japan Society of the UK from 2013 to 2019.

Also by Soji Shimada in English translation
The Tokyo Zodiac Murders
Murder in the Crooked House

A full publication list of all of Shimada's work is available from
www.redcircleauthors.com

One Love
Chigusa

Soji Shimada

Translated from the Japanese by
David Warren

Red Circle

Published by Red Circle Authors Limited
First edition 2020
1 3 5 7 9 10 8 6 4 2

Red Circle Authors Limited
Third Floor, 24 Chiswell Street,
London EC1Y 4YX

Red Circle
www.redcircleauthors.com

Design by Aiko Ishida, typesetting by Danny Lyle
Set in Adobe Caslon Pro

ISBN: 978-1-912864-10-2

A catalogue record of this book is available from the British Library.

Homage to Osamu Tezuka
(1928–1989)

One Love Chigusa

Chapter 1

In the year 2091 AD Xie Hoyu caused a major accident on the expressway. He careered on his motorcycle into the opposite lane, straight into the oncoming traffic, flying into the air and colliding head-on with numerous passenger cars. All the drivers had their automatic driving mechanisms turned off.

Xie's body was crushed, torn to pieces and scattered around. But luckily his head and torso, containing his internal organs, held together in their original form. The neck connecting them was severed, but his insides remained intact despite becoming part of the debris spread around the crash site.

In the old days, resuscitation would have been unthinkable in such a horrendous situation. But, by chance, an ambulance crew was passing and within three minutes the body parts were gathered up, attached to a saline drip, connected to a life support machine and transported swiftly to an Ontogenical Technology Unit (OTU).

Fortunately, there was little damage to the brain and the internal organs. Machines were used to compensate for those essential areas where functionality had been lost. Two prosthetic arms were attached from the shoulders, two prosthetic legs were connected to the thighs, artificial muscles and lungs were utilised, and synthetic blood was pumped around the body through artificial blood vessels. Only the skin was regenerated – from the top of the head to the tips of the toes – using the original organic material. Doctors and AI engineers worked together, with cutting-edge technology and materials, to restore Xie's body to its condition before the accident.

Since part of the brain had been damaged, devices were inserted into the frontal lobe and the cerebral cortex. The eyeballs became lenses made of resin and a mechanical sensor provided the capacity to smell. Xie became a patient with an unprecedented number of mechanical parts. But he was only 25 years old, and it was hoped that, if he could get back his physical and mental strength with a year-long rehabilitation programme, he would be able to get used to his new, cyborg body and use it freely.

As the doctors and engineers expected, after Xie had been in hospital for about two weeks, he recovered his locomotive functions. He could walk normally and, if he had to, run almost as fast as he had before the accident. He could eat as well as a healthy person; his eyesight, ability to understand what he saw and mental capacity were all at the same level as before. At least that is what Xie believed.

His memory had also been restored to its previous state. The five or six years of Xie's recollections which were in the hippocampus and the permanent visual memory secured in the cerebral cortex and the cerebellum were copied onto a Quantum memory drive and handed over to him. There were naked, moving images of a lover in all of this: he was given strict orders not to reveal it to others. And so, through the surface of his visual memory and the huge quantity of moving images, Xie could recall perfectly who he was, what his name was and what his profession had been. With current science, however, the engineers explained, it was not yet possible to recover all his memories, especially the non-visual ones like touch and smell.

A month passed after the accident. The locomotive function mostly stabilised and reflexes such as blinking and chewing returned. He was now able to do all these things without thinking. The constant pain that had ravaged his whole body disappeared. Appetite and the desire to work came back. He started to have cravings. He wanted to look at flowers, at beautiful landscapes, at the starry sky and the expanse of the sea. But for whatever reason, the desire to gaze on a woman's face wasn't there. In fact, he had no desire for any human company at all. There was a TV in the hospital room, but he didn't feel any special compulsion to switch it on. Xie wondered if he had become a person devoid of all passions.

He asked the doctor about this and was told that it was possible to develop areas where functionality had been lost. Using his IPS cells and sequencing they could start replacing them. But it would take time and quite a bit of expense. Negotiations with the insurance companies would be tricky. And it would be extremely painful as well. Additionally, there was no guarantee that the full functionality he had before would return even if these replacements were made. The verdict was that the overall capabilities of each region would probably end up lower than now.

As he listened to all this, Xie opened his eyes wide in shock. Not because of what he was being told but because of what was happening to the doctor's face before his eyes. While he was speaking, the corners of his lips tore open,

3

spreading upwards towards his ears, and his face gradually turned blue. He no longer had the attributes of a living human being. Xie stared and slowly began to shiver.

Eventually, Xie looked down, unable to raise his head. The fear of the doctor's face moving into his field of vision was so terrifying that all he could do was focus on the pattern on the floor. Gradually he noticed that the conversation had stopped and that silence had fallen. It seemed as if he was being asked what he wanted to do. The doctor was waiting for a decision. He had to answer quickly. Without thinking, just to get away from that place, Xie shook his head from side to side. That settled it; Xie's IPS cells would not be replaced.

A nurse with a bright red face knocked and entered the room. Xie was astonished. He fixed his gaze on her for a while. He began to wonder if there was something wrong with his mind or whether she really had a face covered in red pigment. Furthermore, the nurse's eyes were pulled up and her eyebrows – left and right – loomed massively. She looked angry.

With some irritation, she took out a map of Greater Beijing that she was carrying with her and indignantly began to explain the main features of the city and the location of the OTU.

He knew all that, Xie thought as he listened to her. But she pointed out all the public transport lines on the map and explained how to get access to them. She told him how to buy a pass-card so that he could get through the ticket gate and, if that was too much trouble, how at the town hall you could get a microchip implanted into the palm of your hand. He was told that listening to all of this now might seem obvious and something he might feel he knew already, but if he went there unprepared he would only end up becoming disorientated and confused.

After this, the blue-faced doctor came back into the room and said that it was all right for Xie to leave the hospital. But because there was a danger that he might fall unexpectedly, he needed to take great care while moving. 'You've got an extraordinary number of devices in your body,' the doctor said. 'You'll need to attend rehab classes at least once a week for the next year.'

Xie left the technology unit and anxiously went outside. Many images from the Quantum memory drive came into his mind as he wandered awkwardly around the streets with his newly-acquired mechanical legs. He was surprised when the area around him suddenly went dark. He looked up and saw that a stupidly large floating object had appeared in the sky above him.

It was like a horrible manta ray that you find in the depths of the sea: it seemed, terrifyingly, to be a giant object obscuring the sky. It must be coming after him from some unknown star, he thought desperately. And then he suddenly remembered – the images on the Quantum. That was it. It was an earthly vehicle: a Municipal Theatre Bus.

The bus was lifted high on pillars floating from rails buried in the centre of the road, so it could run independently of all the congested traffic down below. Like a giant dish or a distinctive balloon-shaped parasol, the weird passenger bus could travel back and forth many metres above the cars travelling below on the ground. And the bus stops along the way were in the sky too, up flights of stairs from the pavement below, many of them on the second floors of shopping malls or theatres. It was rare to find a bus stop on the ground, and to get on and off the

5

bus people had to use steps that extended out from the bus itself. Usually it was easier to use the stairs.

Xie did not want to use public transport, so started to walk to his old haunts. He'd intended to do this when he left the hospital. But as he began to walk along the pavement, all at once he was startled. He stopped and stood completely motionless.

Faces, faces, faces of people coming towards him. All of them red, just like the nurse he had seen in the hospital. Everyone coming and going in the street, all with strange red pigments on their faces. And all with the same angry expression as the nurse.

Everyone was angry. Faces like red-black demons, rushing past each other. In amongst them he spotted people with ordinary faces, but they were extremely rare and moved very slowly compared to the others. Men and women – but particularly women – constantly passed each other, baring their teeth and emitting moans like wild animals. He thought that if there was the slightest body contact, a quarrel might just flare up and quite possibly someone would end up getting killed.

But Xie had no memory of any such killings. Because they weren't among the data contained in the Quantum. All he had was a terrible feeling of discomfort and fear, as well as loneliness. In an instant, he lost the confidence to live in this city.

You can quickly learn how to use machines, but there were things you couldn't get used to. People. Walking past people – that was the most frightening thing. He couldn't even walk on the pavement unless he averted his eyes from the people passing by. It was as if he had come to a city on a strange unknown planet at the far edge of the universe.

Each day, while looking at his Quantum data, he'd lain in bed doing his 'image training'. He suddenly recalled the place where he used to live and his room. He walked there, opened the door with his key-card, went inside and looked round. His whole past life rushed back into his mind and he felt it almost physically return into his body. The smell of dust and sweat and – almost as if covering it all like a mantle – a strong smell of paint. Through a small window, a view of the dreary city. At his feet, on the white carpet, the fragments of a coffee cup lay scattered, and a black coffee stain remained.

He was instantly hit with a feeling of unbearable monotony and despair. He realised that he just had to try to get through it. He gathered up the pieces of china and threw them into a foul-smelling rubbish bag. The stain on the carpet was unlikely to come out. It had been caused by Tin, his lover, just before he'd left the flat, when she'd thrown the cup on the floor. The incident had all started when she had changed her mind about something she had promised. Or maybe, Xie thought, it might just have been a difference in what they remembered – he didn't want to blame her. But even so, she had found some trivial reason for mocking him. He couldn't remember exactly what the problem had been – something to do with clothes? She had argued – unreasonably – that she'd changed her mind because of Xie's thoughtlessness.

He'd exploded on the spot. It was the unfairness that Xie couldn't forgive. Right in front of him. On so many occasions she had manipulated the circumstances, changed the subject, dodged the truth – it had happened so often. He had slapped her face. Tin had shouted at him, thrown the coffee cup on the floor and stormed indignantly out of the room saying, as a parting shot, 'It's over'.

7

Xie sat down on a chair. He slowly recalled the whole scene. He didn't want to remember even a small part of it, but the memory flooded back of its own accord. Tin had been important to him. But her personality, her unreasonableness, the multitude of petty excuses she would come up with to justify her behaviour – he couldn't put up with it. He had thought it would end at some point. And when the time had come, he had jumped on his motorcycle and headed off for the expressway – furiously opening up the accelerator, full of confusion and despair.

When he switched on his PC, there was an email from the boss of the publishing company he worked for asking him to make contact as soon as he was out of the hospital. As soon as he saw it, tiredness closed in on him. All day long, as he'd walked from the hospital to his apartment, he had been filled with a feeling of despondency such as he had never known, and the thought of going to the office was overwhelming him.

Xie was an illustrator. He made his living working for fashion, youth and interior design magazines, drawing women's portraits – faces and figures – to order. He'd felt the limitations of this work for a long time. Perhaps these everyday feelings of being superfluous had been transmitted to Tin as well.

Had he wanted to die? He'd used to think that if he died it would probably be at high speed. Maybe he wanted to die because of his broken heart. Or maybe it was because he loathed his work. Day after day the physical weariness had reached a peak, until that day everything just piled up. He had continued to feel that he wanted to change and do something different. But when he had asked himself what that actually was, he just didn't know.

8

His boss was a man, but he nagged like a woman. An image floated before his eyes of an office packed full of women. There was no doubt about it – every one would now have the red-black face of a demon.

Xie didn't just draw pictures: he also wrote poems and short copy which were placed alongside the pictures to complement and enhance them. He was as good at this as he was at drawing, and he enjoyed doing it as a sort of speciality – poetic expression alongside these sorts of compositions.

The illustrations were coloured using software that could recall the types of technique and colouring he'd used. But this sometimes looked primitive, so he also used art materials, including brushes. This took time but Xie liked it rather better, because new things emerged in the process.

When he left university, he'd become a newspaper reporter. But after three years, he felt uncomfortable – he just couldn't get used to the crudeness of the job – and he had resigned.

Even so, becoming a magazine writer didn't reduce his sense of discomfort. This didn't suit him either. He disliked the brazen approaches and pressurising of people that the magazine wanted to cover. He disliked being chivvied in his work by his boss. He needed about a week, undisturbed, to draw in a really relaxed manner and to be able to render a person's character. You never had that freedom doing commercial art for magazines: relationships with people were complex and the clients were always making a nuisance of themselves. Little by little, this too became hateful. It wasn't just his relationship with Tin. Everything at that moment had felt awful. He had felt like he was hitting the wall.

But now he had come back to this room, sat on the sofa and reflected, he realised that all the women he'd had relationships with had been like Tin, more or less. Whatever he said, they screamed, got angry and thought only of themselves. A girl who was gentle, had a nice personality, didn't have a temper, and was restrained and mild-mannered – he couldn't ever remember meeting one like that even from his days as a child.

He went back outside and it was just the same. The women passing on the street, the women on the Theatre Bus – all with faces like demons, all equally angry. They didn't express it out loud but felt it silently within – they alone were the victims. That feeling, that sense of being trapped, that this was happening to *them*, that everyone was hurting *them*, that thought – it couldn't have come across more clearly.

But if, revolted by the red-black demon faces, he lowered his gaze from their throats to their chests, what he saw there was that their bodies were all mechanical. He hadn't noticed it before but now he saw it clearly. Indicators with red figures, floating, could be seen through their clothes, their displays constantly changing – amounts of money going up and down without a moment of rest.

And if he looked up at the buildings in the distance, the letters of the displays and the neon signs scattered on the walls and the rooftops would suddenly start to change to numerals. Some changed slowly; some fluctuated violently. The figures looked like the price of something. Were they stock prices?

All of a sudden, a terrible noise began to reverberate. There was a metallic sound, and a chorus of people's cries. It gradually grew louder and louder, unimaginably so, as if it was stretching out towards infinity. He wanted to crouch so that he could block his ears with his knees. The volume rose relentlessly; a mighty sound, irresistibly loud. Xie had to squat: he couldn't take any more.

People jammed together; a deluge of jeering laughter. Gradually he understood. *Close your ears, keep your head down, stay squatting for a while; the noise will end.* Xie then took his hands from his ears, calmly lifted his head and the image-world of the Quantum drive returned and he could see all the passers-by in the form they had had before his accident. People were walking with calm expressions.

It was a miracle. He was cured; the sickness had been cured. So Xie thought. And he began, slowly, to walk again but, in an instant, it became clear that he had been mistaken. Only the men had regained their normal faces. The women were unchanged: eyebrows lifted, red skin, looking like furious demons.

He went up the steps at a bus stop and boarded the bus that had just pulled in. Inside the bus, it was like a theatre. A crowd of passengers were in their seats, gazing, motionless at a screen located in the direction of travel. Short movie sequences – news, a show, some commercials for new products, among other things – were being shown. While watching the passengers, Xie tried to squeeze sideways towards an empty place, behind the back of one seat and past various people's knees, when he inadvertently trod on a woman's toes. His actions were still a bit clumsy.

'Sorry.'

Xie's apology was immediate, but the woman glared at him with a hostile expression. Her eyebrows – both left and right – twitched frighteningly. Her eyes arched upwards too, full of hatred. There wasn't a hint of tolerance for anyone's mistake. *Inhuman*, he thought. *An evil spirit or a creature from another planet!*

It was no different when he got off the bus – the women on the pavement had the same devilish expressions on their faces. He was tired of being scared and he was thirsty. He stopped at a stand on the road selling juice. The women inside were just the same. They looked dangerous. The paper banknote Xie held out was taken, and some small change dropped on the counter.

He tried to remember the neighbourhood from before the accident, despite being dependent on memories from the images on the Quantum. It hadn't been like this in the past. There had been kind women then. Since the accident the neighbourhood had changed. No, the neighbourhood hadn't changed. It was something *in him* that had changed.

He couldn't go on like this. It became difficult to breathe. He couldn't find the right rhythm to inhale or exhale. He went to grab some water in a paper cup. But swallowing water had also become difficult. And as he became impatient, unable to close his airways and his throat, he found himself choking. He started to cough violently and fell forward onto the counter. He thought that he had struck his forehead on the aluminium board. What was happening to him? It seemed as if he couldn't do even the simplest things. As if his appetite, which had been second nature to him up till now, had disappeared just like a light snowfall melting in tepid water. His self-confidence and will to live had evaporated and was replaced by a sense of complete isolation. As the loneliness and dread became intense, he began to feel nervous about how he could sustain the basic reflexes required for existence.

At a time of crisis, loneliness is not good. He'd taken a psychology course at university, and learnt that living beings need a comfort zone, an oasis where there is a chance of companionship and love. And humans need friends. If you can't communicate with someone, you have no chance of overcoming loneliness and insecurity. If there is nothing holding negative feelings back, emotions run out of control. One might even end up on drugs. The problem in Xie's case was that even before all of this, back when he'd had the accident, there was no one – no friend – who contacted the OTU to enquire about him.

Not only was a girlfriend out of the question now, but he had no male friends either. He got on another bus and went out to the suburbs alone. If there was no oasis, at least he could walk through the forest, and bathe in its atmosphere, for therapy. He suddenly craved the chance to walk amongst trees and gaze at a wide expanse of water.

He followed a mountain path as he looked for the shade of a tree. As he sat down beneath one, on the grass bank by the side of a lake, his heart finally started to feel calmer. He knew he should have come here earlier. The peacefulness before him. The water as far as the eye could see. A slight breeze that created ripples on the water. The green of the trees on the far bank. So many yellow flowers in bloom all around.

With a feeling of relief, Xie took some deep breaths. Taking care not to think of horrible things, he closed his eyes. He tried to recall his favourite pictures, images and symphonies.

Something approached overhead. Were they migratory birds? He noticed them with surprise, as they hung for an instant in the sky over the lake. No, they weren't birds. They were a flock of strange, glittering machines, imitating the flapping of wings and flying with their own sources of power.

He felt cold. There was an unpleasant metallic noise, a ringing coming from somewhere. He saw everything in a flash. The cliff behind him was in fact made of grey metal. Xie's latent memory had allowed him to see this all as real nature. But the truth was different. Metal the dull colour of lead, iron reddened with rust, all piled up together. He had mistaken this for the cliff face. Broken pieces of warped gears on top of one side, all stuck together.

A strange object was moving awkwardly on the ground. A round trunk, shining like dull silver. A mechanical creature. But not a living thing. Its body was covered in metal needles, waving backwards and forwards, undulating as it ran, making a shivery metallic noise. It didn't stop there but went on across the ground from right to left.

And now, as far as the eye could see, the yellow flowers and the green grass had suddenly lost all their colour and changed to dull silver. The green completely disappeared – the area around him turned into yellow desert.

The forest on the far side of the lake disappeared. The bare mountain was just desert stretching away. The lake had disappeared. It was just a shallow concrete swimming pool.

All around on the sand stood piles of cold, shiny iron rods. Was this the shadow of what had once been vegetation? To the ends of the earth, lifeless, all changed into a desert of sand and scrap iron? Yes, this was the reality. What he had observed up till then was an illusion. Xie realised that he could now see everything for what it really was.

Chapter 2

Going to the office was something of a relief. He felt as if he was at last returning to being a normal working person. When he looked around, half the office staff looked as they had before. Someone raised their arm to him in greeting. Grinning, he gave a slight bow in return, but it was a person he didn't recognise. He couldn't remember them and it was a face that wasn't on the Quantum.

He walked slowly through the office and everyone's eyes followed him. He found it annoying but no more than that. He made his way to where the boss was sitting.

'You took your time, Xie,' the boss said. 'But your body seems to have healed. You look in better shape than before!' He twisted his lips in laughter, as if he'd said something intended as a joke.

At that moment, the boss's face instantly changed. His skin suddenly became transparent. All his teeth were visible. And his horribly creepy skull was completely exposed.

When Xie lowered his line of sight away from the boss's head, he could see on his chest, underneath his clothes, an indicator board, displaying red figures like amounts of money, floating there. The numbers being displayed were changing dramatically, going up and down.

'Paying for those medical costs must be tough, Xie? Are you in the insurance scheme?' the boss asked with a thin smile.

'Yes, I'm insured,' Xie replied. 'But I'll still be in debt,' he added.

It made him feel he was on the receiving end of charity. He guessed that speaking in those terms made the boss feel good: he was the type that took pleasure in the misfortune of others.

Sure enough, the figure on his indicator gleamed and started increasing. The boss was delighted. Was it denoting the value he put on this conversation or his self-determined value in the office?

'Okay, Xie, you'd better get on with some work.'

Having said this, the boss turned round and called someone's name. He looked back at Xie and nodded firmly.

A scary woman leapt up from her chair and rushed over to him. She was wearing a figure-hugging bodysuit.

The boss gave Xie a USB memory stick and a sheet of paper with a rough sketch printed on it, and instructed him to draw a fashion illustration using the woman as a model.

Xie pointed in the direction of the studio and went ahead of her down the corridor. The woman followed him reluctantly.

He positioned her underneath an LED light and put the memory stick in the computer to display template images that could be used for reference. When he turned to look at her again, her face was red and both her eyebrows were sticking straight up towards a focal point. Just as he had expected, he thought. Until a short moment before, her complexion had been perfectly normal.

She remained silent and expressionless throughout, but after a while, in a surly manner, she opened her mouth.

'I hope you're not expecting me to smile,' she said.

'Whatever,' Xie replied. Maybe if she smiled, her money counter might go up, he thought. Or perhaps the number changed depending on what clothes she wore. The more revealing the outfit and the more on display she was, the higher her number – through the roof, if she takes everything off. Of course, that's why the indicator was needed. Perhaps the effects of speech and action were being measured as cash values. People without religion, ideology or faith, only trust money as the measure of worth and value.

It didn't matter for him either way. A smiling face would not register on his visual cortex. And the odd thing was, even if he tried to imagine her naked, he just didn't feel anything; no desire for her in the slightest.

He fixed his gaze on the girl's angry expression and began to draw the fashion sketch with an electronic pen on the computer screen. Because there was no need to take it too seriously, he turned the support software on.

While she was holding the pose, the girl began, flickeringly, to exhibit the body of a machine. When he suddenly concentrated his eyes on her, she changed back into a woman with tight-fitting clothes. But if his gaze wandered, she returned to machine form again.

Xie drew the girl's body, taking care that his illustration didn't become an image of a machine. But he had to do this manually – because for whatever reason the girl's body had become more consistently mechanical and he couldn't rely on the software.

After about three hours he'd completed the work. He sent the model away and went back to the office to present the picture to his boss, who examined it doubtfully. He looked up.

'What the hell is this?' he asked.

'It's the model, isn't it?' Xie replied.

The boss lowered his gaze again to the picture.

'Is that how you actually see that girl?' he asked.

Xie peered at his work. The girl's face and body had been drawn properly. There wasn't anything funny about it. So he replied, 'Yes, it is.'

The boss's head became skeleton-like again. Xie heard a sort of mumble: 'What am I supposed to do with this?' His teeth were clamped shut, but his inner thoughts could be clearly discerned. The figures on his chest started sinking rapidly. 'Look, Xie,' he said. 'Why don't you go back to your apartment and take it easy for a while? You're looking a bit tired.'

Xie got on the Theatre Bus and returned to his apartment. But he couldn't settle and didn't feel like sitting on his chair or his bed. He stood with his hands fixed to the wall for a while, considering what he should do now.

He'd lived here like this before and now he'd returned and found it changed. If there was a god, he needed to send Xie a message explaining why he existed, what his purpose was and how he should keep on living in this world. What reason was there? He wasn't capable of anything.

Xie Hoyu returned to the hall once more. He put his shoes on. He went down the stairs, crossed a dirty alleyway, passed through a street of shops and walked towards a coffee shop that had been one of his regular haunts in his college days. He entered, stopped at the counter to buy a coffee and walked towards a seat at a table along the back wall. It was the darkest part of the shop, where he wouldn't be noticed. The faces of all the customers, backlit against the large glass front, were dark and their expressions indiscernible. It helped calm him down.

He thought about taking off on his bike and finding a place to die. Although this was no comfort to him, he wondered whether it would be better to die somewhere deep in the mountains, where nobody lived. However he looked at it, there was no relief other than this thought. He had just decided that that was what he should do when – out of the blue – he saw a miracle.

It was in the dirty world, beyond the glass shop front. Suddenly, at the edge of the window, coming from the left side, something out of this world appeared, something unimaginably beautiful – it was a slender woman.

Her figure was lovely. Xie tried to control his feelings so as not to hold out too much hope because she might also turn out to have that red face and terrifying expression. He watched her, absently. The woman looked straight ahead and walked slowly across the world on display through the broad glass front, as if in a panoramic photograph. She was wearing a tight skirt that stopped just above the knee, showing off her beautiful legs and elegant deportment.

At that moment, a child on the pavement just next to the coffee shop began bashing a tin drum which hung from his neck. The real miracle happened at that moment. Surprised by the sound, she turned in his direction and smiled sweetly at the child.

In that split second, Xie was thunderstruck. He opened his eyes wider. The world stopped. It was as if the air had been sucked out of the coffee shop, making him breathless. He almost fell off his chair and grabbed the seat-cushion with both hands in panic.

What a beautiful sight! Xie wanted to shout out. The look she had given at that moment was in a different league, from another dimension, something so different to all the other women walking to and fro in the street. Kind and gentle, like a flower blooming in the gardens of paradise – that was what Xie thought. It was no exaggeration. If a creature of that kind of beauty existed, this is what she would look like. At that instant, for the first time since the accident, he felt strength flooding through his body. Despair left him. Now he wanted to go on living if only for a few more months.

What was the difference between her and the other women? If someone had asked him this, he'd want to be able to answer. Her eyebrows were not pointing up, her eyes were not angry, her lips were not knotted in a grimace, her complexion was consistently fair, and when her expression changed it did so in a relaxed and gentle manner, with a fleeting smile.

Xie noticed that he was standing up. He just couldn't sit still any longer. *Who is she?* he wondered. *Who on earth is she?*

Such a wonderful face! Here, in this rubbish dump, was a woman of such purity – so gentle, looking with such kindness on the world around her. He hadn't realised that this was possible. *If this* – Xie felt like gasping – *if this is real,* he thought, *I can keep going. I can stay alive for a little longer!*

Xie ran, stumbling, across the coffee shop and rushed out into the street. Standing on the pavement, he looked to his right, the direction in which she had been walking. But the woman was nowhere to be seen. The street was packed with nothing but the bodies of people going home from work, as far as the eye could see.

Xie dashed off from the coffee shop entrance in the direction that the woman had gone. He thought he could catch up with her. A woman couldn't walk that fast. As Xie passed women walking on the street, he looked at each of them. But they all had red faces and returned his stare with grim looks.

Where was she? Where was that woman? He felt desperate. *What is my reason for living?* If he couldn't see that beautiful face just one more time he thought he would scream. But wherever he looked, left and right, all the women who caught his eye had red demon faces and eyebrows pointing up. The street at sunset was full of hostility and spite.

Xie ran for several hundred metres, but he quickly became out of breath. He couldn't follow her for one more step. He stopped, bent double, gasping for breath. He crouched in pain. Then gradually, as he got his second wind, his body recovered and he was able to take deeper breaths. He remembered the doctor's words – he shouldn't overdo it yet.

He started to walk on, step by step, passing all the people walking along the road. He couldn't give up so he resumed the search. After all, earlier he'd taken the decision that he was going to die. But the minute he'd seen her that decision had melted away like the mist.

At that moment, death seemed far away – and it was because of her. Did that mean he would die if he couldn't find her? Had that beautiful face, her gentle appearance, seemingly not of this world, become his only reason for living? He didn't know who or where she was. This was completely crazy. But it was undeniably the truth.

However far he went, there was just wave upon wave of people. He merged into a crowd of countless workers, unable to find that beautiful woman again.

Chapter 3

Xie was able to work. But instead of going to his office, from that day onwards he went to the coffee shop each day, took the same seat and waited for the beautiful woman to pass by. That particular seat was not a popular one because it was dark at the back of the shop, so it was always available when he arrived.

Xie stayed there for hours, drinking coffee after coffee. He avoided looking at the faces of the customers. His eyes were fixed on the front window, as he ordered refills every hour. If he had gone to his own apartment, he wouldn't have been able to focus or think of anything to do. Without seeing her again, his determination to end it all just got stronger.

There was no doubt – for Xie, coming and sitting in this shop and looking out through the glass to the world beyond was an effort to stay alive, to distract his mind from pulling him in the direction of death. And his purpose for living now was to wait there for her to wander past, outside the shop window. Xie was now alive because of the beautiful woman he'd caught sight of that day. She was living somewhere in this neighbourhood.

He felt like a fisherman – waiting, all day, his line just touching the surface of the water, waiting for a fish that there was no chance of catching. The truth was that even if he carried on sitting there for a whole week, the image of that woman might never appear again on that street.

On rainy days, on windy days, on days when storms lashed the street, Xie came to the coffee shop. He sat and waited for the woman. All night long, anguished, lying in bed, he continued to think about her – he couldn't focus on anything else. Waiting for her to reappear was the only thing he could think of doing that had any meaning. So he came each day to the coffee shop. The inside of his head was like an empty box.

His tendency to suffer from insomnia just got worse. Mornings would come without his having been able even to enjoy as much as a nap. Perhaps it was because he wasn't doing anything that was physically tiring. That was what he thought, but what was he to do?

On those mornings, he slipped out of bed, left the apartment and tramped through back alleys full of rubbish, stomping over waste paper and litter. And then he would realise that he was standing in front of the coffee shop. His feet never took him anywhere else – whether consciously or unconsciously, he couldn't tell.

He always chose his usual seat. It was always free. He didn't want to sit anywhere else. With a cup of coffee in his hand, he could stave off the intense drowsiness he felt. Nonetheless, when he got back to the apartment, he wouldn't be able to sleep. So it was better to stick it out here at the coffee shop.

Then, suddenly, he heard a raised voice. The same scene, just as before, began to unfold again in front of him. As if it were a film on playback, from the left side that beautiful woman came into sight. Taking long steps and gliding almost gracefully, she walked slowly from left to right across the glass front of the shop, again as if in a panoramic snapshot.

Xie leapt up from his chair, crossed the floor of the dimly-lit coffee shop, and rushed towards the entrance and out onto the pavement. Today he'd reacted immediately. So the elegant back of the woman was still in view. Xie was in a desperate hurry to catch her up.

'Excuse me!' Xie said in a loud voice as he stood in front of her, as if to block her way. In that position, he got a proper look at her face. It was a real shock. Even looking at her close up, nose-to-nose, she looked the same. Her good looks were absolutely unchanged. And he'd never in his life seen such a beautiful face.

'I– I–'

Standing in front of such beauty, Xie was lost for words. She had stopped and was looking at Xie's face without speaking. Her appearance was innocent. She had a look that was not clouded with worldly desires.

She is looking at me now, Xie thought. *No one else, just me.* That alone gave him the feeling that he was ascending to heaven.

She stood there waiting for Xie to speak. Because Xie was quite flustered, almost gasping for breath, she smiled gently, as if to reassure, even encourage him. With a delicate movement of her neck, she inclined her head slightly. The lovely smile that flickered from her lips was indescribable. Her beauty was incomparable. She didn't scowl, she wasn't angry – she just waited calmly for Xie to speak. Xie felt her calm presence.

He was close enough that if he stretched out his hand he could touch her. With deliberation he continued to gaze at her face. Everything began to change; the world around him began to dissolve and her smile disappeared.

Fair, smooth, beautiful skin. *Oh, this skin is alive, it's breathing.* He could see soft, fine hair floating, touched slightly with makeup from her face. This, he knew, was the beauty of a woman. If you look intensely and closely at something of real beauty, when it is at its peak, even if you get only the briefest of glimpses – that beauty just deepens.

Neither her eyes nor her eyebrows were pointing up even slightly, the tender smile again playing around her lips as she waited. Words of anger and wounding, he knew she would never utter. The sheer goodness of her character was evident. Xie opened and closed his mouth desperately, like a fish gasping for air.

He thought: *I have got to do this right. I don't want to upset her and make her hate me! This is a matter of life and death. If she leaves I won't be able to go on living. This is the only alternative to death!*

'I– I was waiting…'

No other words came. He heard a quiet sound of annoyance. Slowly, she opened her mouth. Xie didn't understand why or what was happening, but he found himself staring blankly at her. She was asking him something.

'What's going on?'

It was a reasonable question. How could she understand? So Xie spoke, quickly.

'You.'

'What?' She tilted her head, as if she didn't understand. A faint smile floated around the edge of her mouth. He realised that she was confused by his answer. Encouraged by her smile, Xie summoned up the strength to continue his explanation.

'I've been waiting – right in the back of this coffee shop – for days and days, to see you appear again, on this street.'

Now the woman also had an open-mouthed expression.

'For *days*?'

'Yes.'

'For *me*? Why?'

The sound of her voice really surprised him. It was fine and high, a sweet sound like a bell.

'Why have I never seen a woman like you before?'

At these words, she frowned and looked surprised. But she didn't say anything.

'There is only one woman like you in this city. Really – you are the only one. I was amazed, and emotional, I didn't know what to do, I thought – I just had to see you one more time, I just wanted to see your face.'

She stared at Xie's face, waiting to hear what he would say next.

'All the women in this town look like demons. All of them have scary, red faces. It terrifies me; I can't even look at them directly. But you're different. Your gentle smile, your soft expression. Beautiful and pure, not like a creature of this world. I think a person like you – is a real woman.'

Xie blurted this all out in one breath – this mass of words that he had been storing up in his heart – and then he slowly exhaled.

'Yes?' she said, tilting her head a little. What a charming expression! The sort that you would never tire of, no matter how many years – decades even – you watched it. He wanted to be with her. Even for just a minute or just ten seconds.

'You are the person I want. My ideal. Please tell me your name.'

He bowed his head because she didn't reply for a while. He said, pointing with his right hand, 'Couldn't we talk a little? In the coffee shop? You and me…?'

'What's this coffee shop called?' she asked, to his surprise.

'Eh?' Xie was startled by this question. 'The name…' Even as he spoke, the words dried up. He felt a slight sense of shock. He'd been going there for years – since his college days – but now he couldn't remember the name, no matter how hard he racked his brain. 'The name…' Why had she asked that? What did it matter what the coffee shop was called? The name that mattered was *her* name. That was much more important.

'Can't you tell me your name?' Xie implored her.

'My name?'

'Yes.'

'Why?'

'Just to know your name, your name alone – will be a blessing, a sort of charm – it will enable me to live – to endure anything this ugly world throws at me.'

'It's better if you don't ask my name,' she said. The smile faded from her lips, and her voice became low and cold.

'Why?'

'I have a husband. He does not allow me to tell my name to strange men.'

'Oh…' Hearing this, Xie felt everything before his eyes go black. In a flash, all the strength drained from his body. His knees gave way. *Of course*, he realised – she was married. Despair flooded over him so intense that he couldn't stand. He found himself kneeling on the pavement.

'Married…' he mumbled. If he thought about it, of course it made sense. A beautiful woman like that would not have been ignored by the men of this world. 'Oh – well

27

– it can't be helped…' He forced the words out. 'Look, I don't want to go out with you – I don't even want to drink tea together. I just want to know your name.'

'My name is Tin,' she said in a voice that was a little harsher, raising her face in surprise. Then the white face of this gentle, beautiful woman changed suddenly to red and black. Her eyes, left and right, twitched upwards, and she morphed into a different woman – one slamming a coffee cup on the floor with a scream like a devil. The woman he had split up with.

Xie was amazed. She cackled with the sort of shrill voice you would use to call animals.

'Loser!' she shouted.

Everything he saw turned dark, as if it were night, and his field of vision gradually became distant and detached. Slowly he bowed down, until his hands were spread out and touching the cold pavement. It was all as he had thought. The time when there was a reason for him to keep on living was over.

Xie woke suddenly from his nightmare.

Tears poured from the corners of his eyes; he sobbed uncontrollably. Eventually, he fell back into a short sleep as dawn rose.

Chapter 4

That night, Xie tossed and turned until dawn. He slipped out of bed when the sky was still a light red and went – almost crawled – to the coffee shop, sitting in his usual seat. It was already open and serving breakfast for labourers. He had started going there earlier and earlier. What else could he have done except stay in bed? And there he wouldn't have been able to sleep.

Outside the glass window, a mother and child were walking across the pavement from the left hand side. The child was a little boy, probably in kindergarten. Xie watched without really looking. Suddenly, the boy shook off his mother's hand and slipped free. Xie wondered why such a young child was walking along this street so early in the morning. Dangerous, he thought, but not unexpected.

Then the little boy fell over badly. A young woman passing by at that very moment spotted him, crouched down and gently picked him up, holding him from behind. It was like a silent scene in a film being played out beyond the glass shop front.

The little boy – feeling himself being gently lifted up – began to sob. Raising his face as he cried and turning his head, he saw the face of the person who had picked him up.

Realising that she was smiling, the child instantly stopped crying, as if frozen. He was taken aback and sat down on the pavement. It was as if he had seen something unexpected and unpleasant. So frightening that he was incapable of continuing to cry.

Xie turned his head to watch this tough little child's reaction. The expression on the boy's face seemed to be one of extreme fear. What was the terrible thing that he saw? Intrigued, Xie also looked at the woman who had picked the little boy up and held him to her. He had the same reaction. Shocked, he fell from his chair. But in Xie's case, it was not because he was scared. It was because she was the beautiful woman that he had been waiting for, day and night.

Of course Xie stood up immediately. He rushed across the floor and towards the door with all the energy he could muster. He'd been waiting for her for a month. At last he was going to meet her. Yes, at last she'd come back! These words swirled around in his mind. He felt so happy. He'd never imagined that she had to get to work so early. No doubt this was why he hadn't had the chance to meet her.

He'd consoled himself by thinking that she didn't actually exist. But in his heart, he'd constantly daydreamed about the moment when he might meet her. He'd thought that it would have been enough just to see her face. He hadn't hoped for anything more. Throughout that empty month, he'd nurtured that wish each day.

Xie hurried towards the cafe's exit while still looking through the window. The child's mother was approaching – as expected, with a face that was bright red and had a crazy look on it. She glared at the woman who had picked her child up with an expression of utter contempt, as if she

30

thought the woman had been trying to steal him from her. She took her child, turned her back and hurried away from her as quickly as possible.

The young woman gave a solitary smile. Slowly, she rose to her feet, turned and walked away. At that precise moment, Xie Hoyu rushed out into the street. He would be able to catch up with her. She had been crouching, and that meant that he had enough time to reach her.

He followed her, trying to draw level with ever faster steps. If he continued at this speed he would soon overtake her, so he slowed to a walking pace. He had remembered his dream – and the dream's tragic conclusion. Who could guarantee that this dream had not been a premonition?

He lost all power in his legs and hips and couldn't increase his speed. That horrible feeling he'd tasted in the dream – he would experience it again, he couldn't stop it; there would be no escape from its utter foulness. If this was all happening to him again now, there was no mistake – it meant it would lead to death.

He walked, keeping a distance from her. What should he do? He had to avoid suicide somehow. He wanted to avoid it by whatever method possible. The beauty of the woman, the elegance of her body, her legs almost dancing in front of him as she walked on. He wanted to call out. He wanted to hear her voice. He wanted her to recognise the existence of a man like him. But his heart was wavering, all because of that bad dream.

Go round her. Face her front on. Bow your head and say, 'Good morning, nice to meet you'. *Give your name. Ask for hers, straight out.* 'Where do you live? What do you do for a living? Where are you off to? How old are you? Are you married? Children?'

He'd fantasised about doing just that a thousand times. He'd seen it in his dreams. But the result was always the same: misery. The voice he didn't want to hear, the face he didn't want to remember. That dream had been horrible. He often wondered whether he hadn't actually lost the use of his heart and whether it might still be working. But this was no joking matter. His life depended on what he decided to do. This was undeniably the real thing. He couldn't approach it carelessly or casually. He was walking along a cliff edge between life or death, no question about it, and if he fell over that cliff, his 25 years of life would finish. *Carefully, carefully*, Xie said as if he was screaming at himself.

Thoughts raced through his mind. Could Xie be sure that he would not be hurt by this woman? The world was deteriorating rapidly. The news on the Internet was full of terrible incidents. A man whose beloved car was destroyed by his girlfriend with a hammer; a father run over and killed by his daughter; a monstrously obese woman punching and beating someone up on the street; another man robbed of his money and goods and shot with an electric gun; a man murdered by his wife of many years, a sixty-year-old husband who had his bones and internal organs resold… He didn't know when all this had started to happen. Morality seemed to have disappeared from the world. Making money, winning and losing, dog eat dog – these were the principles of survival. And they were being sharpened up. This was all that mattered now. The journey from having a bad experience with a woman to falling into hell itself was a short one. After all, it is society itself that is hell in the first place. But if there was a space where love could grow, a man could find a way out of that hell.

Humankind – why is it organised like this? Why is it that these creatures live and populate this earth? Does all this have any meaning? Sexual reproduction, and creatures that relied on it, was becoming less and less important in a civilisation now dominated by cutting-edge technologies. Humans were no more than faded supporting actors, old-fashioned, with primitive ideas, about to leave the stage. Singularity… In the old days, it was fashionable to talk about that. You never hear that word now. It is never on anyone's lips. Why has that happened?

Yet even in the middle of all this savagery bound up with the origins of life in the world, there was a beautiful and gentle woman. Humans cannot be left alone. It didn't make sense for her to live alone – not to have a boyfriend… Would it be tasteless to ask?

If he could find out where she lived and worked, he could go there every day. He could watch her walking or sit outside the cafe, drinking tea, and watch her go past. That would be enough. *But I've got to talk to her*, he said to himself. *Always running away – that just won't work*. That sort of life would be unbearable. *For now I will just follow her silently*, Xie thought.

Today she was wearing tight-fitting trousers. Not the skirt that she had had on before. So it would be easier for her to run off – although he doubted whether it would actually be that easy for her to outrun him. While he was thinking all of this, Xie took up a position about twenty metres behind the woman and walked onwards with silent steps.

Had they now walked far enough? She turned and stepped into a broad boulevard. Were those gingko trees? They were tall trees which Xie didn't know the name of. They lined the street, stretching into infinity. He walked

33

underneath their branches. The dappled sunshine through the mass of overhanging leaves fell across her shoulders and down towards her hips like a small waterfall. It was a beautiful sight. Just that alone made him feel as if he had been saved.

Xie walked on, trying not to notice the overhanging branches and the countless green leaves, whose colour was unchanging. He didn't want to see all the trees change into silvery metal poles. The image was so unpleasant. Almost sinister. It made him feel terrible. But the weird thing was, with the woman walking there, the row of trees was just a row of trees. Maybe Xie's visual function really only wanted to observe the woman.

Further on, at the end of the line of trees, there was a red brick-pillared gate. Above the two pillars, there was a stainless steel angled arch with 'Shankal Electric' written in the Western alphabet. The metal gate below was shut, but a small door in front of the security guard's room was open, and the woman passed through it into the factory grounds.

A moment later, Xie arrived at the same gate. He didn't want it to look as if he had followed her. When he looked through the metal door into the factory compound, he could see her slim form walking on a path across a lawn, disappearing into one of the buildings on the site. The words 'Lithium Ion' were written on the door. On the building opposite, the words 'Spinning Saucer Battery' were written in large characters in a single circle.

He approached the little window of the security guard's room; an old man was sitting on his own inside. Xie put his face near the window and asked whether he could have a look around the factory. The old man asked why, and Xie replied that he wanted to work there. As soon as the words popped out of his mouth, he felt he had said the right thing. If he were to become her co-worker, there might be a better chance of getting to know her. But then he was told that the company was mechanising fast, so it wasn't looking to recruit people mid-career. It sounded as if at this firm people – humans – were unnecessary accessories.

Looking around the factory wasn't possible, he was told, as they'd recently had the problem of some confidential information being leaked.

When he enquired about a possible news article for the magazine he worked for he was told it would be better if he were to present a business card from his publishing company and then make an official application to the firm's press office. Xie nodded and stepped back.

It would depend on the circumstances, he thought, but it was hard to imagine that a high-concept, modern, lifestyle magazine would publish an article about a bog-standard generator and battery factory. And the boss would never agree to it either.

He decided to ask what time the workers who had just arrived usually left the factory. The guard said that he didn't know – each section would have their own arrangements.

There you go, he thought. If the sales department was liaising with someone on the other side of the world, then it might be late at night or early morning. There's no need for those people to come to work now. If you looked around, you couldn't actually see any people coming in anyway. And production facilities were increasingly automated too.

There's nothing for it, he decided. *If I'm going to see that girl again, I just have to wait until it's time for her to leave.*

Chapter 5

After standing there for a while, Xie sank down on to one of the benches between the gingko trees lining the path. Streets with benches in them were rare, so the thought of sitting had not even occurred to him. Public benches were few in this city. Xie had no memory of having wanted to sit down as he walked around the town. And he didn't particularly want to sit down at that moment. He just thought that sitting down would prevent him standing out. The bench was situated in a dark spot shaded by the thick trunks of the gingko trees. It was difficult to see, either from the Shankal Electric security guards' room, the shops lining the boulevard from left to right or by the people walking by. He thought he would wait like this until noon. She would probably come out then to go to lunch. He wondered whether it might be better to take a seat in the outside area of a cafe, but if he stayed there too long the waiting staff might get suspicious.

If he didn't move his upper body, the sunlight seemed to fall through the mass of leaves and rest upon his shoulders, and the warmth around that part of him increased. It wasn't what you'd call sleepiness exactly, but the feeling of slight drowsiness was coming back, and if he let his feelings go, he felt free, like a kite carried on the winds of Arcadia, fluttering about in a blue sky – not at all unpleasant.

As he felt the warmth spread from his shoulders through the gingko leaves, Xie shifted the weight on his bottom and, leaning back so that his neck was resting on the back of the seat, he looked upwards. The desire to look at the leaves welled up inside him. So many leaves, all piled up and interlocking against the sky. But a question arose. Each leaf was slightly out of position with those around it – which meant that each was exposed to the sunlight. There were so many that it seemed miraculous that each one was able to bathe in this light. It was incredible. How was the position of each leaf calculated? The infinite energy from light created by nuclear fusion generated sugar and glucose in each leaf, allowing these trees to grow to their present state.

If you applied AI to these big trees, in the same way that people separated the young into different groups for purposes of teaching or training, these leaves would be forced to grow straight and in a clear line, like a group of schoolchildren on a field trip to the zoo. If the leaves were stacked like IC chips or solar panels, only the top leaves would be fully exposed to sunlight and the tree would wither away, malnourished.

Xie found himself smiling; indeed he snorted with laughter a little. Was it because the community of gingko trees didn't want to perish, that each leaf individually bore the cost of moving slightly away from the central column towards the light? And did it generate, at that instant, a form of speculation, leading to a kind of duty or tax, creating benefit and interest, a sort of war, even, to avoid reserves being drawn down? Was that it? Behaviour, with its etiquette and sense of virtue, takes us closer towards death.

He'd learned the word 'Arcadia' in primary school. For whatever reason, he'd liked it and memorised it by writing it down over and over again. It was a story he'd heard at that time about an ideal village. A true story from the olden days.

There was a cave halfway up a mountain a little way from Arcadia – a sort of sacred place for the young men of the village. The old people and women didn't go there because the climb up the mountain road was too steep.

If you went just three hundred yards into this narrow cave, a whole world would suddenly open up to your view. This world was a perfectly organised village where everyone lived, in a grand space like the inside of an enormous, upturned, hidden mortar. There was a crack in the limestone that resembled a crescent moon, and through it you could see the tips of the trees on the mountain summit. The falling sunlight created white streaks across the sandy soil. And in that sand, an underground stream was flowing, and when you scooped the water out with both your hands, you found clear spring water without the slightest impurity.

The sand spreading out at the bottom of this bowl was like the desert of western China. On the outer periphery of the space, in front of the wall of the cave, there were countless grey stalactites and icicles stretching upwards as well as hanging from the roof. And there was also a thick stone pillar like an old tree, connected to the wall of rock far above one's head – so big that one person alone would be quite unable to put their arms around it.

If a person saw it just once, they would think it was like paradise – the world one had heard of and would go to after death – an unforgettable, mighty, wondrous sight. Standing here for only a short time, in this immense piece of art fashioned by nature, made you feel that all everyday human activity was inconsequential.

One man amongst a group of men who had come from the village sat in front of one of the stalactites, rubbing its surface repeatedly saying: 'Emma-o, the god of the underworld, is here.' He enquired of the novices around him, 'Can you all see?' They shook their heads from left to right, saying no.

'Here is a face. It's a terrifying face. And here is a hand. Left hand, right hand,' the man explained. Everyone laughed. 'If you just say it like that, we can't say we can't see it, but it's not clear, it just looks like a grey stone,' one of them said.

'All right then,' said the older man to the first one who'd spoken. 'I'll use this chisel to carve Emma-o out of the stone so that you'll be able to see with your own eyes.' He was a man who made his living carving animals and demons from old logs and trees.

'Wait a minute,' a young man at the back of the group piped up. 'Won't you let me have a go?'

'A kid like you?' said the older man, although he didn't dismiss him out of hand. Everyone fell silent. It was because the youth who had raised his voice was the most skilled painter in the village. 'Well, then, can you see Emma-o's face?' the carver who'd first discerned the face asked.

'Yes, there it is, clear as day,' the young man replied. 'Tomorrow, I can start carving it myself with a hammer and chisel, and do a proper job of it,' the young man asserted confidently.

'All right, if you put it like that, go ahead and do it,' the carver said. But – because he was an older man, only after a dignified pause and after thinking – 'Let's give it a week – just one week. A grace period. If, in that space of time, everything goes wrong, I will replace you with someone else. You're a painter: I have more experience of carving. The reason Emma-o is sitting here has to be because of the gods' will. Everyone wants to carve the deity, because their name will live for ever. But I can't let someone who doesn't have the skill do this holy work.'

So the young man who was the most skilled painter in the village brought a lot of candles and bedding into the cave, and every day, by the light from the sky during the day, and candlelight once night had fallen, he battered the stalactite with his hammer and chisel. He never once went back to his lodgings in the village when evening came. If he couldn't produce a splendid work in a short time, someone else would take this precious work away from him.

The week passed quickly, and the older man who had first discerned Emma-o came to look at this work. He fell silent as a splendid portrait of Emma-o was revealed. He could not complain. And, as his companions could not say anything either, the holy work was entrusted to the young man.

He immersed himself in his task; ten years, then twenty years quickly passed. The young man became mature in years. The older men of the village, beginning with the carver, died one after the other. A rumour went round that a bride had been found for the young man during this period, but he was so obsessed with his work that he never noticed her. And as his hands became the hands of an old man, finally, Emma-o was completed.

By that time, the people of the village no longer came to the cave. This was because their attention had shifted to a magnificent Buddhist temple that had been built in the middle of their town. This was now what attracted everyone's interest. Girls of the town, renowned for their beautiful looks, sang and danced and went to the events and festivals held in the temple grounds. No one climbed up the precipitous steep path on the edge of the town to the cave halfway up the mountain any more.

Having expended all his effort on this work, and having made a statue of Emma-o so brilliant and lifelike, the artist was content. Over several days, the man spent his time climbing up the mountain to gaze at the work on which he had spent his career. Because he didn't want it to be damaged by anybody, he brought some wood and built a small shrine to surround the image.

He brought in some saké and, alone, lifted one celebratory cup and allowed himself to smile. But after he had gazed at the sculpture for a whole day, he spotted one little part of it which dissatisfied him. It was the base of the little finger of the god's left hand. It looked thick, as if it was swollen. So he opened the door outside the image of Emma-o, went inside, up close, inserted the tip of his chisel at that place and struck it with his hammer.

He was supposed to be highly skilled but perhaps the problem was that he was drunk. His actions were a bit rough and the little finger broke off from its base, fell into Emma-o's lap and rolled over making a rattling sound.

The man gave a mighty scream, enough to fill and shake the whole cave. He stood motionless, in terrible despair. Something unbelievable had happened. Everything had gone perfectly up till that point. Why had he now done *this*? With one last stroke, the masterpiece to which he had dedicated his whole life, on which he had laboured unceasingly, was now ruined.

He tried to endure this despair, but it was useless. There was nowhere he could escape. There was no convincing story that made it all right for Emma-o to have no little finger. He had given his whole life to making this statue of Emma-o, and now it had all come to nothing. His life had become worthless. Slowly he fell to his knees, bowed down and cried out in grief. The gods and goddesses of creation had deserted him.

He kept on crying until the sun set. Then, when it was late, he stood up, staggered down the mountain, and on his way back to the village, threw himself into a dark lake whose surface was illuminated by the clear brilliant moonlight. And there the man died.

Xie had understood this story even when he was a child. He felt the man's despair. And when he became an adult, his understanding became deeper. He loved painting, and his compulsive inclination towards work that revealed some divine inspiration meant that he felt the man's fate more painfully. If he had spoiled something on its day of completion, he too would probably not have wanted to go on living.

Under the gingko trees, he had become lost in the despair of the tragedy of that long-ago artist, but as the sunlight crept through the gaps between the leaves and fell on his shoulders, warming his body, he began to feel good about himself, like in the past. This helped to restore his spirits and rescue him. And so he didn't change his posture but stayed sitting on the bench.

A curious noise brought him back to his senses. He turned his head, looking left, then right and then behind him, and saw a great crowd of people walking down the tree-lined street which, until then, had been completely empty. Most of them were men, but there were a number of women too, all with red faces. They were all wearing workers' uniforms, so there was no mistaking the fact that they were Shankal Electric employees.

Xie, hurriedly, searched for the form of the beautiful woman in the crowd. But however hard he focused his eyes, he couldn't find her. It seemed that she was not there. So Xie turned his gaze and held it on the entrance and exit next to the security guards room. If she were to appear, it had to be from there.

On either side of the tree-lined street, there was a row of shops – an electrical repair workshop and small restaurants selling Mediterranean food, coffee and such. Xie heard a strange kind of music, probably coming from one of those shops. It had a Middle Eastern melody and rhythm that he wasn't used to.

While he was listening absently to the music, Xie continued to watch the gate by the security guards' room. A short time seemed to elapse but the factory workers had finished their lunch in the little restaurants and began to return to the factory through the small gate on which Xie had fixed his eyes. The midday break was over. The quietness he had experienced before returned. He was disappointed. She had not come out for lunch at all.

He closed his eyes, let his shoulders droop and continued to listen to the music still coming from somewhere. There was nothing to be done. If it was going to be like this, he would just have to wait until the evening hour came – until she left the factory to go home. There was nothing else to do. It wasn't so hard, so he decided to stay there.

He suddenly – unexpectedly – realised that he was hungry. When he thought about it, he realised that he hadn't eaten anything since the evening. Because he'd begun to feel a little better lately, his digestive system had been working normally and that was probably why his appetite was now returning. Xie turned his head and looked at the restaurants, wondering which one he should enter. He decided to go to the one from which the sound of the exotic melody was flowing. It was a Persian tune, the sort of melody that Arabic people liked. Xie also liked this sort of melancholy music, so he decided to have some Mediterranean food, for the first time in ages. He was getting a little fed up with eating Chinese.

He stood up, crossed the bicycle lane behind him and walked up a quiet footpath. After walking about thirty yards in the direction of Shankal Electric, he came to a place with a sign reading 'Kebab and Falafel'. He stood and looked at the shopfront where the names and photographs of the dishes were displayed. Then he had a strange feeling. Xie realised that the volume of the music should have been getting louder as he got closer to the source. But the exotic melody that he could hear was unchanged – no more than a gentle sound.

Xie went through the narrow entrance, bowing his head. But again the volume didn't change or increase. He stopped, a little confused, unable to go into the gloomy interior. He bumped into a table by a large glass window stained with oil. The inside of the cafe was deserted: there was no sign of any customers. The busy period was clearly over.

The manager, a man with a Middle Eastern-style black beard brought over a glass of water, and Xie ordered a kebab wrap. 'Chicken or lamb?' he was asked. He replied, 'Chicken.' The manager was thickset with dark eyebrows.

In only fifteen minutes, a kebab wrap arrived on a metal dish decorated with a red and purple floral pattern.

With a ripping noise, Xie tore open the dry-looking paper and bit into the chicken kebab. At that moment, almost as if on cue, the Middle Eastern music that had been playing suddenly stopped. And–

'Electricity, electricity…' a male voice – nasal, as if under water – repeated. Then, after a slight pause, 'Benjamin Franklin, Benjamin Franklin,' it continued.

What? Xie thought as he ate his lunch. *What is this? What are you trying to say?*

The voice stopped. There was silence for a while. Xie waited anxiously. Then–

'Thunderstorm', the man's voice said, continuing in a murmur, 'Thunder. Kite, kite, kite. Thunder, electricity, kite, Benjamin Franklin.'

'Thunder, electricity, kite, Benjamin Franklin,' it repeated.

The meaning wasn't clear, and Xie stopped chewing, as if in a daze. He stood up and looked out through the glass window.

'Thunder, electricity, kite, Benjamin Franklin,' he heard the man's voice repeating.

He could see some people walking down the avenue. Five or six men. But they were all walking calmly. It didn't look as if they could hear anything. They didn't seem to be looking around to see what was happening, or behaving as if it was anything untoward. Could it be that they couldn't hear it? Why was that? Xie wondered: was he the *only* person who could hear this voice and that melody?

'Thunder, electricity, kite, Benjamin Franklin.' Still he heard it. Even when Xie blocked up his ears to see if it made any difference, the noise was still there. Was it ringing in his brain?

As Xie watched the receding figures of the people walking, the manager came and stood near him.

'What's up?' he asked, looking at him suspiciously, with a strange, goggle-eyed expression.

He's asking me? Xie thought.

'What is it?' Xie muttered.

'What's the matter?' the owner asked.

'Can't you hear that noise?'

'What?' said the owner.

'That. A man's voice. Saying "Thunder, electricity, kite, Benjamin Franklin". Can't you hear it?' Xie asked as the voice began again.

'Can't hear a thing,' the manager said, shaking his head.

'Yes, that's it', Xie muttered. *Of course: it's only me that can hear it.* 'It's okay. Thanks,' Xie said.

He dropped back onto the chair. The tone of the voice had changed. It was stronger and clearer.

'Aryan. Aryan.'

Chapter 6

After he'd paid for the chicken kebab and left the cafe, the melody began again. Xie walked slowly while he was listening to it, crossed the bike lane, turned right under the gingko trees and, after wandering for a while, found a bench that was out of the sightline of the manager in the cafe. He sank down on to the seat. When he leaned back and let out a sigh, the music, mysteriously, stopped dead.

Silence. As he sat there, not moving, he heard in the depths of this quiet a slight, metallic noise: an uninterrupted ringing. Like a wire stretched upwards to the sky that sounded as if it was whistling in the wind in mid-air. Was it some form of tinnitus?

The road in front of him was wide but there were no cars passing by. Once you had reached this point there was nowhere to go apart from into the Shankal Electric site. So no throughway for vehicles other than those delivering ingredients and other items to the cafes and shops lining the street, perhaps? Without that business, there'd be no cars coming here at all. So that's why it was quiet.

He listened intently. It wasn't a pleasant sound but it wasn't uncomfortable or unbearable either. While listening, he recalled the voice of the man he'd heard earlier and thought he should try to understand its meaning. Because somehow he had a feeling that he *could* interpret the melody that had been ringing in his ears. And the reason was, firstly, that all proper nouns were included within his memory.

'Aryan,' the voice had said repeatedly, *hadn't it*? This must mean the so-called Aryan people, a people linked by the archaic Indo-European languages they spoke. Or perhaps it meant the 'Aryan' race – a term Xie knew was steeped in controversy.

When he was at university, there had been a professor who had lectured on what he called 'Aryan history'.

Xie scanned his memories. The Aryans, the professor had said, had originally been nomads who lived in the grasslands on the northern shores of the Caspian Sea. Twice they had been dispersed in population explosions (the origins of which were apparently unclear – in two thousand and some hundreds of years BC and again some hundreds of years later). Some believed they had gone to Europe, the Middle East and to India, and apparently either scattered the people who were living there, or massacred them – in any case, over time, taking control. Ferociously violent behind their intelligent appearance, they were said to be extremely good at waging war. Well, that was what Xie could recall from his professor's lectures. But he knew that many people objected to the word 'Aryan'.

In the 19th and 20th centuries, more than 150 years before Xie was born, the phrase 'the Aryan race' had taken on a new and ugly meaning. It had been stolen by people who believed in racial purity. It had led to some people being dubbed Honorary Aryans and much more besides. There were apparently researchers who'd collected legends like *Noah's Ark* to explain the movements to the south.

But there was also a theory that the Mediterranean Sea suddenly flooded after a violent seismic shock, overflowed into the Caspian Sea, dispossessing them of their lands and triggering the migration.

While he waited on his bench Xie couldn't think of anything else. Then, he began to have strange, intrusive thoughts. Were modern Europeans descendants of these Aryans?

Following the advancement of science and technology in the Middle Ages, and when these new advances reached a tipping point during the Age of Discovery, another period of explosive population growth occurred. This resurgence led to another great migration of people with significant consequences.

The professor had said something about the Europeans being a type of modern Aryans, settling in lands – not just in South America but in India and Australia too – decimating the local indigenous population there on their arrival with the new viruses they brought with them. North America was settled as well and the Indians living there faced a similar fate. Large numbers of people from the African continent were pushed into slavery and forcibly transported to North America.

These were atrocities. Western Europeans took over control as if by heavenly command. Perhaps this was simply 'progress', an epic journey of advancement that was destined for the whole of humankind, and we were all now still in the middle of this 'glorious' history.

That was what began to rattle around in Xie's brain. Not a melody any longer, but more like ceaseless, thumping music as he sat there with his new, mechanised cyborg body and artificially engineered memory trying to grapple with the words he had heard. He couldn't focus his mind on anything else.

As for Benjamin Franklin, Xie recalled that he was an American pioneer, one of the Founding Fathers and a scholar with a British heritage. Did that make him fall within the definition of having 'Aryan' descent, Xie wondered? And whatever did that actually mean?

Advanced modern civilisations were all based on electricity, and electricity had been discovered because of the naturally occurring phenomenon of lightning in the skies above the earth. It was Franklin who captured this energy and brought it down to earth. Franklin had researched the powerful electrical energy of lightning. Then he had collected it from the air using an extraordinarily dangerous experiment of flying a kite in a thunderstorm, thus proving that electricity existed.

'Electricity, electricity, Benjamin Franklin.' That's why the strange male voice was calling out those words: 'Electricity, electricity, Benjamin Franklin.' The voice in his head seemed to be protesting about how humans had obtained electricity.

But why complain about that? Why now? Why was it coming up *now*?

Were these mental images a sort of digital memory recall? Were these thoughts about electricity and the so-called 'Aryans' thoughts that Xie had had before? Now, when he reflected and ruminated on this again, it seemed to him to be the very reason why these thoughts had emerged. If the 'Aryan race' hadn't moved south from the Caspian Sea during the population explosion, the world would have been a simpler place where ordinary people would have lived in peace. Maybe there would have been *some* war but not the massacres that led to many different tribes and groups disappearing from the earth.

And perhaps there would have been no America, no Franklin, no Edison, no discovery of electricity. Bringing that power down to earth would have happened much later, wouldn't it? And this rapidly modernising civilisation, with its forest of skyscrapers and communication radio waves flying through the air, would also probably have been slower to develop. Perhaps these 'Aryans' came into existence on the earth in order to discover electricity, earth it, and develop today's advanced techno-civilisation in the shortest possible time. With the helping hands of The Creator, perhaps?

Or was this just a muddle of misunderstood memories from the Quantum drive, half-remembered definitions and intrusive thoughts?

As a matter of fact, Xie recalled that he had heard that there were still elements about electricity that remained a mystery, even to specialists. The *nature* of electricity is apparently completely understood by humans – which is to say, we know how to harness it, generate it, how to transport it to a distant place. We understand what things to avoid, how to use it to carry out any kind of work, and so on. But he'd also heard that what electricity actually *is*, wasn't even properly understood today. Humankind only knows how to generate it, its basic nature and how to use it.

It was probably the same for Edison, who was lionised as the king of inventors. In his case, he could exploit the mysterious power of electricity in his laboratory for a limited period when he alone possessed the secret. But it was a race against time to devise a way of using this magical power to make useful life-enhancing devices. Edison didn't fully understand the principles of the machines that he had himself developed. But through brainstorming various ideas and intuitions he had managed to continue making discoveries and observe what electricity could do.

Nuclear power generation was similar. It has long been known by scientists that bombs can be made with uranium 235, which causes fission. However, the mined uranium ore extracted from underground is a mineral that is 99.3 per cent uranium 238, from which fission is difficult. Only 0.7 per cent of the remaining uranium 235 is the type that can be split causing nuclear fission. So, in order to make nuclear bombs, it was necessary to refine uranium ore to produce uranium 235 – so-called enriched uranium – with purity as close as possible to 100 per cent.

If uranium 235 is collected inside a weapon in a large enough quantity, nuclear fission will start automatically. There's no need for implosion. You get an atomic bomb like the one dropped on Hiroshima. The reason the nuclear bomb was never tested first was that everyone had known from the very beginning that it would explode with devastating force.

The image of the beautiful girl he was waiting for was no longer there to distract him, and Xie's mind ran on and on, compulsively, continuing to dredge up everything he could remember on the topic, desperately trying to find a meaning, a purpose in it all.

Uranium 235 is very scarce on earth. So it can't be used to mass-produce nuclear weapons. Once uranium has been subjected to fission, the uranium absorbs neutrons and plutonium is generated as a waste product. This can be used to make a bomb. And with sufficient quantities of this waste product, mass-production of nuclear weapons becomes a realistic possibility. This is the type of bomb that was dropped on Nagasaki.

Then it was discovered that this plutonium breeding device was able to generate super-high temperatures like the sun, stably for long periods, and that it would be possible to make a power-generating device through the boiling of water and the generation of steam. This is the principle of nuclear power generation.

In other words, today in the late 21st century, the scientific power of humankind is still a simple, unsophisticated thing. The advancement of science on the axis of electricity was not planned by humans. It was more that humankind has been propelled to this point through the irresistible force of the various electrical machines that have been continuously created.

So why 'Aryans'? Although these people seem to have played a major role in the history of science and its refinement, they would clearly not have borne so great a responsibility if they had not been a masterful and adventurous people. It was this group that harnessed and gained understanding of electricity. Could no other group have managed this unprecedented work? That was a pretty Euro-centric way of looking at the world, wasn't it?

As he sat under the gingko tree, Xie ruminated about all these different things. Were these 'Aryans' created to assume this great task? By The Creator? Or by someone who could make a massive profit by putting electricity on the earth? That voice calling out to him – to him and no one else – was that the great secret? And why was it appealing to him only? *That voice wasn't heard by anyone else. It was just calling me. Why me?* What was happening to him? Was it a glimpse of some unseen power? Why were these intrusive thoughts and muddled memories afflicting him? He clutched his head in pain.

Electricity, perhaps? Xie thought. *Is it because of electricity? Inside my body, there are so many batteries; also a generator. I am unique – the most radical child of this modern, advanced, electrical civilisation. There was no other way I could have survived as a living creature after such a dreadful accident.*

Yes, in his roots, in this living, functioning creature's life, was the essence of these 'Aryans'; Benjamin Franklin, the kite, thunder. Yes, he understood, Xie thought quietly to himself. That's why that voice was there, obsessively urging him to be conscious of all of this.

He sat there for some time as the sun set in the west and the wind grew chilly. How long had it been? As it blew a little stronger, his neck grew cold.

He stayed sitting on the bench, though, as the temperature fell. Then, in an instant, he saw. She was coming out through the factory gate.

Chapter 7

Xie waited for her to pass him on the other side of the road. It was wide enough for Xie not to worry about her becoming suspicious of him, sitting on the bench. He just sat there and watched her walking gracefully along. And after she had walked by, he stood up slowly, crossed the road and began to follow her.

She walked slowly through the city as twilight fell. She had changed clothes inside the factory. She was now wearing a tight black skirt that hugged her body and looked like artificial leather. Xie continued to watch her slender, beautiful legs below her shiny, glossy waist as he followed her silently. They moved forward, together, as if in a slow, delicate dance.

He walked slowly, at the same pace as her, keeping a steady distance. It was strange, but just because of this, he felt a happiness that he'd not experienced recently. He hoped that this moment might last for ever. Even if he died close to her, like this, what regrets could there be? None.

He didn't want to approach or overtake her. For one thing, he didn't actually have the courage to speak to her. Today, it would be enough just to find out where she lived, if he could. The only thing on his mind was to walk with her.

There were no others leaving Shankal Electric. She was alone when she arrived and when she left work. But just as he was thinking this, a wave of people appeared from the left, and she was swallowed up amongst them. Xie was taken by surprise and, fearing that he might lose sight of her, increased his speed. Unexpectedly, he came to within a couple of metres of her slim, elegant back, and his heart began to pound. He was almost touching her. And Xie then was caught up in a whirlpool of weary, work-tired men.

The men didn't speak. They moved silently and quickly. Xie felt their stifling body heat, like being engulfed in a muddy stream; then suddenly the coffee shop was in front of him.

There was a light on inside the shop, so he could see the usual customers sitting on chairs looking at their tablets. There was no one sitting in his usual seat against the back wall. He felt strangely relieved as he looked at it. He felt as if he had returned home.

Then he spotted her again, and in the twinkling of an eye, she turned right into an alley about a hundred metres past the coffee shop, as if to escape the wave of humanity. Xie wondered if she disliked people. She walked on to the end of the alley and then turned left and carried on down an endless, narrow street.

It was full of food shops and general stores selling reasonably-priced goods and groceries, all lined up next to each other, but she showed no interest in any of them. She just carried on walking at a steady pace. There were no other passers-by, so Xie held back a little, keeping his distance.

Eventually, they emerged back on the main street once more, and a movie theatre came into view. She walked up the steps in front of it. Taking care not to get too close, Xie followed her. He could see her attractive legs from below.

Moving out on to the upper raised terrace, she slowed her speed. She was clearly intending to wait for the Theatre Bus. Xie was confused. He hadn't expected this. She stood at the bus stop at the end of the terrace. There was no one else waiting for the bus. If Xie stood alongside her, she would get suspicious. And if he stood behind her for a long time – even if she didn't suspect anything immediately – she would become aware of him and no doubt think it odd. She might even call for help, and then he wouldn't be able to follow her any more.

After thinking about it, Xie concealed himself a few steps down, away from the second floor itself, reckoning that when the bus came he could run out behind her and nip on to it without her noticing. Quite a lot of people rushed up the stairs when they saw the bus had arrived so it shouldn't be too difficult.

She was standing with her back to the stone steps, watching the traffic over the handrail to her right. The sun was gradually setting. A large bus arrived in the empty sky with its lights blaring, and he hurriedly turned the other way. When he looked back at her on the second floor above, she was still waiting at the bus stop.

The bus slowed and headed towards the raised terrace. Xie darted up the steps to the terrace and made a beeline for the bus across the paved space. Buses were driverless, operating automatically, but these self-driving buses were all programmed to detect any movement by people nearby who wanted to get on.

Xie embarked safely. The bus was full and hardly any of the seats, which were arranged in rows like in a theatre, were empty. She walked towards the back of the bus and seemed to lean against a windowless wall. Xie decided that the best way to keep his eye on her was to make his way to a seat in the middle of the bus. He was worried that he might lose sight of her. He sat at an angle, trying to catch a glimpse of her out of the corner of his eye.

Xie glanced at the screen in front of him. But he had no interest in what was being displayed and certainly not in trying to follow and read the subtitles displayed in two columns of Chinese *kanji* characters: he just looked intently at the standing figure of the girl at the edge of his vision.

The beauty and grace of her body were extraordinary. It was odd that the men around her didn't say anything or try to talk to her – such an exceptional woman, so beautiful in appearance, like this, in this city – let alone on this bus.

She began to move. It looked as if she was getting off. Xie moved awkwardly, shifting in his seat as she brushed past the people sitting in his row and moved sideways into the aisle of the bus. And as it pulled into the next stop, she alighted and went off into the dark. Xie followed.

The sun had completely set now and the moon was on the horizon – a dark, reddish-brown moon, almost full. She walked on down the steps behind, out of view, then crossed the paved street and went up onto another platform, which looked like an old-fashioned tram stop. *Was she changing from a bus to a streetcar?* Xie thought, surprised. It looked as if she had a long commute.

Xie was perplexed. He couldn't approach her at the tram stop. So, once more, he hid at the corner of a building and waited for the streetcar to come. Eventually, the lights of a two-car tram came into view, and he slipped out from his hiding place and ran across to the streetcar entrance gate as it pulled in.

He boarded the tram and stood as far as he could from her. Then he held on to a strap. She did the same. The tram was crowded; nearly all the seats were occupied and there were many people standing, hanging onto straps. Commuters, returning from work, almost certainly. There was only one vacant seat, but she didn't sit down. Nor did Xie. He figured that with such a crowd of people standing, she was unlikely to have seen anything that might make her suspicious.

He leaned forward a little and stole a glance at her, standing a few metres to his right. Every time he saw her beauty, he couldn't control the feelings welling up in his heart. Almost overflowing. Looking around the tram, he saw so many men – young, old. But the surprising thing was that none of them seemed at all interested in her.

Why? Xie wondered. *Is everyone blind? Haven't you ever seen such a beautiful woman like this before? Why aren't you surprised at seeing her on this streetcar? Why isn't even one person inviting her out to have a cup of tea? Why isn't there even one person asking to take a photo?*

They were jolted around for a long time. The self-driving tram stopped at so many stations. People got off and new people got on – there was quite a changeover in passengers. Xie and the woman were now the people who had been there the longest. But there was no sign of her alighting. Where the hell was she going? Did she live so far out? What a commute every day. Had she never thought of moving nearer the company?

At that moment, Xie heard the voice of a woman standing behind him. Because the voice sounded a bit hysterical, as if the person was at her wits' end, Xie quickly focused on what was being said.

'Welcome to the world of the common people...' the woman was saying to the man next to her, in a derisive tone. 'I guess this is the first time in your life you've been slumming it on a tram like this, isn't it? I supposed you're used to swanning around in one of your fancy electric vehicles. You know, the ones that come with an audio-system or a drone attached. And now you deign to pay us a visit to have a look before the whole dump gets redeveloped. What do you know about a place like this? The people here live on ten bucks a day, if they're lucky. Even a trip on a tram is a luxury for people like this. Everyone walks.'

'Look, if the place is being redeveloped, it needs an inspection, doesn't it?'

'And I suppose you felt like inspecting me while you were at it.'

The man snorted with contempt.

'Let's get to the point. Okay? Your time is so precious. Isn't it? An hour's worth, what, a quarter of a million? Am I right or am I right?'

'You're not wrong,' the man said.

'How about me, then? I'm gorgeous, I'm smart, I'm elegant, I'm 26. You won't find another like me easily. I've got the looks, the style, the nous, the attitude. The one thing I don't have is a partner to match.'

'So we're talking money, are we? I'm just a wallet as far as you're concerned? Look, do me a favour. I'm getting off at the next stop. I have a car waiting.'

'You're just walking out on me?' the woman said in a high voice.

'It's over. Right here, right now, on this tram. You want some friendly advice? Find yourself a job that pays good money. Don't waste all your time looking for a man. You'll just end up in pointless arguments like this. Find a job, build up your assets, you can take your pick. Who knows, *you* could even keep *him*!'

The man raised his right hand and headed for the exit door. 'Call me if you need a lease,' he said as he got off.

The woman he had left behind continued to stand silently in the tram. As far as Xie could tell from the indistinct reflections in the dark glass, the women in the crowds all constantly passing each other still had their red faces.

As he was standing there with his back to her, Xie thought about what had just happened. Maybe the woman was doing the same, although she might have come to a different conclusion.

He thought about why he had followed the woman from Shankal Electric and was now standing there on a streetcar. It was so desperate that it was painful. Was he stalking her? He didn't see it like that. He felt overwhelmed with the sense that he had lost his way. As far as the case of the woman behind him was concerned, her motives were crystal clear; there wasn't any doubt. But what *he* wanted wasn't at all clear. It was elusive; there was no way of understanding it. If this was what they call romance, love, what was the point of it?

His peripheral vision had become hazy. But he saw that the woman he was following was now walking towards the exit of the tram. And Xie found himself, sluggishly, moving as well. Although it was as if the energy had completely drained from his body.

Chapter 8

It was the sort of night in which gentle music could be heard. The hard sound of her steps was continuous, like the mechanical rhythm of a drum. The white moonlight shone down as the sound reverberated through the various back streets. If he listened as he walked on, it all became entwined, a little like the sound of the strings of a jazz guitar, echoing languidly.

Xie continued to slow his pace. A sense of futility steadily occupied his mind and overwhelmed his feelings. He couldn't find any meaning in his actions. His body was without energy. Even that was meaningless. What he was doing, like everything else, was completely pointless. No matter how many times you talked about 'meaning'. And now he'd come here, he finally understood what impression the woman would have of him if she knew he had followed her for so long. He realised that what he was doing – the disgusting way he was behaving – couldn't make her feel good. Of course, he hadn't imagined it would please her, but now he realised what an unpleasant and pointless thing it was.

As the woman opened up a wider gap between them, her elegant back and beautiful legs melted into the darkness of the night. Soon the distance from her would become infinite. It was at that point that he would have to give up his quest.

As Xie realised this, he heard the sudden noise of a boisterous, cheap bar. Unexpectedly, this jolted his nerves – which had become dulled – back into life. It didn't appear to be a high class establishment and he felt as if it stained the purity of an evening suffused only by moonlight. It was unpleasant. He was surprised. It was such a vulgar din and he thought she would walk straight past it. But, as if issuing a direct challenge to the noise, she walked straight up to an entrance that looked like a dark hole next to a shop with various small, red neon signs on display.

Xie was shocked: he stopped still and looked at her back. *Do you actually want to enter a dive like that? I'm sorry to see that you do.*

But without any hesitation, she walked up the three stone steps and vanished into the darkness of the entrance.

Dazed, Xie stood still in the street and he thought about the reason for this turn of events. It was harder for him to understand than the row between the assertive woman and the rich man on the tram. It strained his ability to think it through; he felt under pressure. It didn't seem the sort of place that a beautiful woman, who seemed so pure and transcendent in every way, should be going to. It was old and dirty. It was the sort of place that the people the poverty-stricken woman on the tram was talking about – living on a few bucks a day – might go to.

Xie slowly walked towards the dark entrance. Reaching it, he walked up the stone steps – yes, three – then, still in earshot of the noise from the bar, he touched the wall to his right and peered into the darkness. Then he had another surprise.

Xie had thought that it was the entrance to the bar, but it wasn't: it was just a dark corridor. There was a stainless steel mailbox on the left hand wall. It was an old box but it had three tiers, with countless openings – in other words, this was an apartment block, and these boxes were probably for the mail for each of its residents. But when Xie looked closely at each of the mail boxes, there were no residents' names, just a list of the names of engineering companies – XX Works, XX Contractors, XX Pipe, XX Steel.

He went a little further into the corridor. A small lift with a scratched door was on his left, with a staircase beyond it. There was an electric light on the landing of the staircase, so a dim light fell across the first floor. There was a switch on the wall of the stairs and, when he flicked it, the white LED lights embedded in the ceiling all came on. Xie immediately felt he had done something wrong and turned the switch off, throwing the area back into darkness.

Somehow suppressing the sound of his footsteps, Xie went a little further along the corridor. There was another lift, with a double door, larger, with dents all over the place and even more battered. The corridor got wider and pretty dirty, but eventually a space that looked like a lobby came into view. And, after passing through all this, there was a large entrance. It appeared that there had once been a door there, but it was now gone. On the wall there was the trace of a hinge, and on the floor a hole where a pillar had once stood.

There were three stone steps at the door, leading out onto the street again, facing a wide entrance. He realised that the door through which he had entered was actually the back door. He went down the steps, stood on the street and took in the whole scene, turning his head right and left. He could see quite a long way because of the streetlights ahead all along the road. But there was no sign of the woman in either direction. She had completely disappeared. *No, maybe that's wrong,* he thought. *She's gone back to her apartment in the upper floors of the building. She's gone to her room, tired out after a long day's work, and right now she's unwinding.*

He went back up the steps to the pitiful lobby. He wondered if he had pinned down where she actually lived. But there was no sense of achievement and he started thinking about what he should do. It was all very different from his imagination, and all he could feel was disappointment. There was no neat little cafe with seats outside in this neighbourhood. There was no place where she might be seen, elegantly sipping coffee.

He retraced his steps, cut through the corridor, left by the back door and returned to the alley. From there he searched for the entrance to the bar on the right hand side from which a discharge of alcohol-oiled voices and noisy music was leaking out. He walked along the wall; the entrance was at the corner of the building. All the small windows in the bar were open, and the racket was pouring out into the alley.

With the full force of his body, he pushed the door. The noise was explosive. He felt as if he had been un-ceremoniously punched in the face. Looking around inside the bar, there was a white mist, almost a fog, and it was dark as well. He had a bad feeling. It seemed to be misty because the customers were smoking, and although this had apparently encouraged them to open the windows, this had produced no obvious improvement in the air quality.

A number of girls wearing thick make up were showing off their legs and dancing in the aisles. The men were sitting on chairs, smoking cigarettes and beating time as they watched, cheering raucously. In the intervals between the songs, everybody burst out talking at the tops of their voices. With their rough, crude language and violent appearance, the people looked like animals, and their threatening looks – if turned in your direction – inspired fear. The men were waiting for the music to begin again, and for the women to approach them as they danced, so that they could touch their bodies.

Xie approached the counter and asked a bartender who seemed at a loose end if this building was an apartment block. The barman was smoking a cigarette and knocked the ash onto the floor with a hand sporting a blue tattoo before saying that it had once been apartments. Xie asked what they were now. It was a warehouse. And was that true of all the rooms? Most, thought the barman. He'd heard that there were offices too. Again, Xie asked if there were people living here. The barman thought not. During the day stuff was taken in and out. Who would want to live in a noisy, filthy place like this? Would you? Xie replied that he wouldn't. The barman asked if he wanted a drink. Xie said he was okay and left.

He walked for a short while, then sat on a bench further along the street, crumpled up his body and stayed quite still. He didn't adopt that position in order to think about anything in particular. He just stayed like that for long enough, no thoughts coming to his mind, clutching his head with both hands and feeling a dim sense of shock. There was no harm in reflecting.

He thought about what he had to do next. But no matter how hard he concentrated, nothing came to mind. He thought about everything that had happened to him since he had returned to his flat from the OTU. Going to the coffee shop, seeing that beautiful woman and forming the illusion that he now had a reason for living. He hadn't thought it through. He'd just followed her to this place. But when he'd realised that what he was doing was absolutely selfish, simply for his own benefit, those original thoughts returned to him. It was like starting over again, with a blank sheet of paper, on which he could write – nothing.

Something had changed. He didn't just feel empty now, he felt desperate, because he was confronting something worse. He was worried: he had to get to the bottom of this and stop these feelings. He held his head and thought about it a little more. He did this for a long time and slowly began to understand.

He had become a person whose existence was of no use to anybody. It was half a year since he'd left the bed in the OTU. Had it taken all that time for him finally to realise this? He was a life-form that, in the eyes of humanity, meant precisely nothing. As he realised this, he cried at the futility of it all. He had lost his way; he was at an impasse. He had not willed this. He had been led astray along a lost road that had no ending. The only thing left for him now was to find the proper way to destroy himself.

It wasn't simply that he thought he'd been stupid. In the final analysis, he'd been such a narcissist. Following that woman, moment by moment, had been such an intense time for him he hadn't been able to think of anything else. Doing it had given meaning to his life. Even if someone had whispered to him that this would kill him, he would have gone on doing it – make no mistake. So it wasn't that he had any regrets. But he had to admit that there had been, well, a misunderstanding. Not about his following her, but about his own life, his existence and what it meant for him.

Despite it all, he decided to go to the tram station and started walking along the cobbled road. That was when it happened. Xie was astonished and stood bolt upright. An impossible sight appeared before him. Was it an illusion? He caught his breath. A beautiful spectacle, not of this world, was there in front of his eyes, by the wall, alone and waiting.

She stood in profile, her leg bent slightly and placed on a block. Xie froze and stood motionless. *Why?* he asked himself.

The moon was now shining brilliantly above the roofs and illuminating the alley. Xie suspected that she might be an illusion of the moonlight. He was sure that she was. If he approached, she would disappear. He couldn't help but move closer to confirm this. But he was terribly scared as he did so.

The closer he got, the more intense her beauty became. It was unbelievable: as he approached her, the intensity grew uncontrollably. Infinite, limitless, it grew and grew. She was a miracle, flawless, perfection. She was a creation touched by the gods.

She inclined her head down a little, bending slightly. Eyes downcast. Long eyelashes. She stayed still, just like that. Her face was white, not a hint of red. And there were no figures floating on any indicator across her chest.

A beautiful vision before his eyes. Why was it a vision? Was he dreaming again? Because she herself had no idea who he was – Xie Hoyu.

She doesn't know that I have been following her. There's no reason why she should be waiting for me. And yet, isn't it clear that this vision has been waiting for me? What is this if not a miracle? It must be true.

No, it's all too simple, Xie thought, as he finally began to work it out. He started to use his head. *This situation is the same as before. I'm seeing a dream. It's just a dream. And if that's the case, I'm ready for the unhappy ending. There are only a few more illusions left to see. Let me imprint these images on my mind. But I shall hope for nothing.*

Slowly, slowly, Xie approached the woman. He was about two metres from her. Slowly, she raised her face and opened her eyes. Xie had the impression that he could hear the secret sound of her eyelashes rising. Surely that couldn't be? And – ah – she released a sigh. How beautiful she was! He couldn't help but bow his head. He was convinced she was going to disappear. But when he looked up, the miracle was still there. She hadn't disappeared. And she appeared – she really appeared – to be smiling.

Xie had stopped breathing. It was that much of a shock. But it was definitely from joy, not regret. He could collapse and die at her beautiful feet. He waited in front of her. Motionless. What was it? Had he died? No, he had just awoken from that impossible dream. And for some reason, she didn't disappear. She continued to exist.

'Why?' Xie murmured involuntarily.

'Eh?' her tiny voice responded.

Xie's heart undeniably began to panic. But oddly enough, the palpitations weren't intense. He wasn't exactly calm, but he was coping. And he was able to form words.

'Are you waiting for someone?' Xie asked.

'Yes. You,' she replied straightaway. The softness of her voice was like a dream.

'What? Why?' he said immediately. The words tumbled from him. It was because he was surprised. But there was no response. He realised that he still believed that it was a dream and that allowed him to behave unaffectedly. 'I'm happy – that you can tell me like that – I'm truly grateful that it was me – but – why me...?'

She seemed to be pondering this. It was as if she didn't know how to answer.

'Do you live here? Or hereabouts?' he asked.

She shook her beautiful face from side to side and said: 'I don't – live…'

Her high, delicate voice! Oh, how could it be so adorable? Why was it such a beautiful voice? Just like the voice of an angel.

'But why – in this place…?' Xie couldn't continue with what he was saying. He didn't want to admit that he had committed a criminal act in stalking her.

She lifted her face and said, 'You followed me for a long time. I was scared. I worried that something might happen to me.'

'Ah—' Xie said. He froze and fought an urge to collapse. She *had* noticed. He'd frightened her. He'd done something wicked. To scare a delicate creature like this, walking around the town by herself at night – why had he done such a terrible thing?

'I'm sorry. I did something awful. I apologise – I'm ever so sorry.'

'I went into that building and waited for you to disappear.'

'I'm truly sorry. I didn't want to do anything to you—'

'So why did you follow me?' She looked straight at Xie as she asked him.

'You were so beautiful…'

'What?' she said, sounding surprised. 'Beautiful? What is beautiful? What is that?'

'Eh?' On hearing this, Xie tilted his head. He was shocked. He didn't know how to put it another way. What was she saying? She didn't seem to understand the greatest compliment of all. 'But why did you wait for me here like this?' he asked. He couldn't understand what had just happened.

'You were crying. So I waited.'

'Crying? Because I was crying?'

'Yes. If you cry, I have to wait.'

Xie felt calm. But he still didn't understand.

'Well, thank you. How kind you are. How different from all those women with scary faces walking through the city! You're my ideal. My dream. A dream – and a reason to live.'

'Yes?' she said, raising her head. She had a quizzical expression and a mysteriously, utterly irresistible face. She continued to stare at Xie Hoyu. No words were spoken.

Xie also stood still, looking at her face. Delicate skin, beautiful eyelids. Below her eyebrows, little cavities, throwing a shadow. And long eyelashes. Beneath these – big black eyes. Fine, white, beautiful skin. A high, thin nose. The eyelids on both sides were a light pink.

'I don't understand,' she said, sighing as she uttered the words.

'Oh, I'm sorry.' Xie wanted to express his feelings and thank her for seeming to listen to him. They were both saying things that the other didn't seem to understand. But this opportunity might not happen again. It was a chance, even if they were talking at cross purposes, and he wanted to take that chance, however slight, of communicating his thoughts. And he wanted her to remember him, even for only a moment.

'I'm not going to live in this world much longer,' Xie blurted out.

'What's that?' She looked up, with a suspicious, just-as-I-thought expression.

'I saw you outside the coffee shop. Through the glass. I was aware of you, and I couldn't forget you. Every day, every day, I thought about you. Not a moment of rest.' Xie lowered his head as he said these words. He couldn't see

71

her expression. He was scared to know how her eyes might react. 'You think that this is an exaggeration? It's the truth. You have become the god of my salvation. The ultimate god of my salvation – because it's so difficult to go on living. Sounds ridiculous, doesn't it? But it's the truth, it's the absolute truth. Wherever you are living in this world, I can also be alive.'

He glanced up at her. She looked pensive, her eyebrows knitted together in worry.

'I'm sorry, I still don't understand what you mean.'

'It's crazy, I guess, what I'm saying?' Xie said involuntarily, with a bitter smile.

'I've just never been told that before.'

'I understand. But I don't need *you* to understand. I just want you to hear my story.'

'Listen? Me?' she said, as if surprised.

'Sure, right now. Or a little later is fine, but I want you to hear me out.'

'What? Is that what you want?' she said, even more surprised.

Xie took a deep breath. As he listened to her, he began gradually to feel as if he were approaching the pool of death. He didn't know why, but he felt he had no will of his own. In gradually growing despair, he had the illusion that he was summoning up the courage to fling himself from a cliff. The moment that had seemed like a dream had finished. And finally, because this night would not come again…

'Are you married?' Xie asked at last. It was the question he wanted to ask most. He had fantasised about it – he had asked it in his dreams, too many times to count.

Now the words were out of his mouth; Xie closed his eyes tight. And waited. It was the moment of death.

'Yes?' The woman seemed surprised again, and her voice was suspicious. Her expression also seemed one of doubtfulness. But Xie didn't see this because he wasn't looking at her. And this surprise seemed the biggest of all.

'I'm sorry if I've shocked you. I've been very rude.' Xie apologised properly, bowing deeply, his eyes tight shut. In that position, he opened his eyes slightly, keeping his gaze fixed on her shoes. 'I'm so, so sorry. Finally, I met you. And finally – finally – I was able to speak to you,' he said while he stared at her shoes. His voice gradually dwindled into a whisper. 'I'm in a dream. I panicked. I understand myself. So… it's okay. If you're married, just tell me clearly. It would be all right just to see you from afar, to yearn for you: I could serve you in that way. I could live like that from now on. I wouldn't care. Are you… married?'

'I'm not married! It's because – I can't—' she said, in an oddly firm tone of voice. At that moment, Xie leapt a metre in the air with joy.

'You're not married!' he shouted in delight, and began to dance around in the street. 'Honestly?' he asked again.

'Yes.' For whatever reason, she sounded angry. And her expression gradually became one of suspicion again. 'Why…?'

But Xie was not listening to her words. 'Oh, what a wonderful life!'

Not heeding her voice and expression, he smashed his palms together violently. Then he clasped his hands, shook them fervently in front of his closed eyes and bent down a little as the tears flowed down his cheeks.

The woman didn't seem to understand Xie's behaviour. But it wasn't long before she realised why. He wasn't focusing on what her face was doing. He was too bound up in himself. For Xie, this was the greatest joy he had ever felt in his life. He could not recall anything like it.

'Thank you, thank you!' he cried, bowing to her over and over again, tears falling on the paving stones.

'That's...' She began to speak but seemed unable to continue. Xie thought that that was strange. But he was so excited.

'Oh, yes, I'm so happy. How much more joy could there be in this world? At this moment, I really feel I'm in heaven. Do you know what I mean?' he asked.

'No,' she said regretfully.

'What's your name? Won't you tell me your name?' Xie asked breathlessly, as if aware of his pent-up excitement. She opened her mouth vacantly.

'Name? My name?'

'Yes, your name.'

'Why?'

'Why...?'

'Do you want to give me a command?'

'A command? Me? You? Why? What could I ever *order* you to do? I'm looking at a god. You are my god. I want to sleep with your name inside my heart. You are my goddess. I want to live murmuring your name over and over again, for ever and ever, in my heart,' Xie said, almost screaming. 'All the time, all the time, all through the day, I will never get tired of it. If I can do that, I will be happy. When I wake up, when I am walking through the town, when I am eating, when I am drinking coffee – all the time. Always, always, I want to be murmuring it in my heart – your name. This will save me. Just your name. Please. Tell me.'

'Name...'

'Yes, your name. When I call you, I need to know your name. Please try to understand.'

'Everyone calls me Chigusa…' she said, as if embarrassed.

'Chigusa? Chigusa? Is that Japanese?'

'Yes, it is.'

'Chigusa – are you Japanese?'

'Eh? I don't understand. But – I guess so.'

'I'm Xie Hoyu. Do you live around here, Chigusa-san?'

'No, a long way away from here.'

'Ah, you came all this way to keep zig-zagging away from me as I followed you, I suppose.'

She made no reply. This was concerning.

'I'm sorry. I've put you to a lot of wasted effort. Please – let me take you back, close to somewhere near where you live. Of course, I won't do anything. I won't hold your hand or put my arm round your shoulder, or touch you. Look. Like this. I'll walk slightly apart from you. Not right to where you live. If you don't want to tell me where you live, somewhere near is okay. After all, it's my responsibility; I made you come all the way out here.'

Chigusa stood there silently.

'Let's go, Chigusa. Please believe me. I'll never do anything to you. I swear to heaven – I'll never harm you.'

Chigusa began to walk. Xie walked alongside her, out of the alley onto the road with the electric streetcar tracks. They approached the tram station and got onto a tram that soon pulled up.

Xie was uncontrollably happy. When they had been on the tram earlier, she had been a person completely unconnected to him. Now they were together, travelling side by side on the same tram.

'When I got on the streetcar before, there was a super self-confident woman, and I was standing right next to her,' Xie said.

'Yes, I remember,' she replied.

'You remember?'

'Yes, she was really beautiful!'

'You must be joking! You're so much more beautiful,' Xie said. She looked surprised and examined Xie's face. Xie repeated what he'd said: 'You're more beautiful!'

Chigusa looked confused and didn't seem particularly happy. But at that instant, Xie, who had been euphoric, suddenly recalled the thoughts of despair that had seized hold of him earlier. He had become a mere presence – a ghost – of no benefit to a living, breathing, reproductive person such as this woman. A life form without any meaning for her. As these thoughts ran through his mind, he grew suddenly cold.

Chigusa said she would get off the tram. Xie followed. She walked down the road towards the Theatre Bus stop. While walking alongside her, Xie was surprised. This was quite a long return journey. Now they were approaching the area where he lived, he could see that he had taken her on quite a trip.

They approached the terrace, opposite a mall, where the bus stop was situated, Chigusa silently climbed the stairs. Was she going to get on this bus? It was a route which would return them to the vicinity of his apartment.

'Thank you. You trusted me. Please let me accompany you to somewhere closer to where you live,' Xie said.

'Yes, I do trust you. You are not a strange person, and not a scary person.'

'Quite the opposite. I will never harm you. I will do anything for you. I want to protect you,' Xie said.

They were now at the bus stop where they had caught the bus earlier. They went quite a long way through the alley and came onto the main street where Xie's favourite coffee shop was situated.

Then she said, 'You don't need to come any further.'

'Oh, okay. You'll go home on your own?'

'Yes, I'll go home now. Thank you for accompanying me. Well then…' She turned her back on him.

'Hey, Chigusa-san, wait a moment,' Xie called after her. She stopped and turned round.

'Yes, what is it?'

'Well – please…' As he spoke, she stood silently. 'This is rude, but couldn't you – well – go out with me? Or not go out, but maybe, once in a while, have a cup of tea? I don't want to ask any more than that. I promise. And maybe – chat a bit…?'

She looked surprised again. Xie became nervous and nodded, 'Is that impossible?'

'To go out? With me?'

'Yes.'

'If we – went out – what would we do?'

'Well, drink coffee, eat? If you go as far as Shankal Electric, there's a coffee shop on this road on the left hand side – you probably know it?'

'Yes.'

'We could go there together…'

'I can't enter that shop,' Chigusa said.

'Why?'

'Why? It's a rule. I'm forbidden by my boss.'

'That's awful. Why, it's tyrannical, an abuse of human rights. Well, there are other coffee shops. We could go somewhere in town, have a meal, go to a movie, maybe…?'

Chigusa stood bolt upright, as if astonished. Behind her, there was just the noise of the wind and the countless electric vehicles going back and forth. There were lots of electric vehicles because it was a solar charging road.

'Chigusa-san, won't you go out with me?'

'I don't understand. I can't reply.' Chigusa spoke as if she was troubled.

'Why? As a friend, just as a friend, that's all. I wouldn't hope for anything more. I wouldn't do anything that you find disagreeable. I wouldn't disappoint you. I wouldn't make you sad. I swear.'

Chigusa stared at Xie's face. 'I don't understand why you say these things to me. Like this, to me. Anyway, I can't. I'm sorry, I am leaving.' Chigusa bowed her head, turned her back and walked away.

'Chigusa-san, I'm going to be waiting for you at that coffee shop,' Xie said in a slightly raised voice to her retreating form. 'I'll wait forever. Forever. No matter what you're forbidden from doing, I can't think of anyone but you!'

Chigusa slowly became more distant.

'That's why every day, every day, all the time I'll be waiting. All the time, all the time, waiting. Just for a little word – that's all, so please come by that cafe. Tomorrow morning, tomorrow evening, I'll be waiting there. So please, walk by.'

'I don't understand,' Chigusa said from a distance as she turned back.

'Will you or won't you? Okay? Chigusa-san? I'll be waiting,' Xie Hoyu said one more time, as Chigusa receded further into the distance.

Chapter 9

For three days, Chigusa did not appear in front of the coffee shop. Xie Hoyu went to the Shankal Electric site every day and walked around looking for her. But he could not find her.

At last, on the morning of the fourth day, Chigusa did appear on the pavement outside the cafe. Xie immediately rushed out of the premises and ran after her.

'Thank you for coming by!' he said, bowing, as he tried to catch her up.

'You asked me to,' she said, turning slightly towards him.

'Thank you,' Xie said, his head still bowed.

'Not at all. Thank *you*,' said Chigusa, looking straight ahead, her head also bowed. Those words alone made Xie feel that he was in paradise. 'For me – someone like me—'

'Why do you say such things? You are wonderful. You are beautiful, like something out of this world.' Chigusa was still staring straight ahead as he spoke, and she looked confused. 'This world is filthy. But your body and your mind are pure, like fresh spring water and air. I can see inside a person's heart. It's like an image. Your heart is pure and virtuous. I don't see anything corrupted there...'

She opened her mouth, as if to speak.

'Don't you understand?' he asked, again.

'Yes. Why do you say such words to me?' Chigusa said.

'Because you should understand,' said Xie.

'Me?' she responded. 'I should – understand?'

'If you are a woman, you should understand.'

'What?'

'That I've fallen in love with you.'

'Love?'

'Yes, love. What is this if it isn't love? I've fallen in love for the first time in my life. From waking to sleeping – although I'm not sleeping that much – I think of nothing but you. Always, all the time, your face is before my eyes, and I am not thinking of anything but you.'

She stood motionless, thinking.

'What is… love?'

'Eh?' Xie was taken aback by what she said. 'Are you joking? Love should be the most important thing for a woman.'

But Chigusa slowly shook her head from left to right and said: 'I don't understand.'

Xie was dumbfounded and stared at Chigusa. Such a beautiful woman didn't know what love was?

'I do not know – love.' The word came out of her mouth, just like that.

'Love – it's like I said – just now…'

'Like the condition that you were talking about just then?'

'Yes, that's right. That's love. It's as if I can't think about anything else, my body can't move…'

'Like an illness?'

'No, much nicer. I didn't understand this feeling until I met you. I knew the word, but this is it, the reality.'

He had known of the notion of love but had always been suspicious of it. He'd decided that it was a phenomenon that only existed in novels. A fiction created by a single beautiful word. He'd thought that love was just a dream, or something from a tear-jerking drama. But he was wrong. This was real. And it was more powerful than he had imagined. It paralysed all his emotions. His muscles stopped working. But the joy it brought to him was stronger than any drug.

He asked, 'Have you ever experienced it?' Chigusa shook her head from left to right.

'No.'

'Aren't you – well – happy, maybe? A little bit happy…?'

'Yes.'

He felt a faint disappointment and he didn't know why.

'Isn't that love…?' Xie murmured. Love was a beautiful, joyful thing, like a heavenly dream – but that was not all. Like the other side of a coin, extreme pain was there as well, fixed like a target to his back. 'Is it okay? Chigusa-san, is it all right if I walk with you, just like this, to the company gate?'

Chigusa walked a short way silently and then shyly nodded her assent.

'Are you sure it is okay?' he checked, gently.

'Yes,' she said.

'I'm glad,' Xie murmured. 'Are you glad?' She listened and nodded. 'So you must be in love.'

'Isn't love a happy thing?'

'Of course.'

She nodded again.

'Of course, it's happy, it's fun,' Xie continued, 'it's the best thing in the world. I guess there's nothing that beats it. But it isn't only joy, it can be the most heart-breaking thing too. Two sides of the same coin.'

'Happy and heart-breaking? Is that – love?'

'Oh, yes.'

He thought about that after he had said it. Happy and heart-breaking. But more than that, it was something that couldn't be explained in words. Whoever you fall in love with, the feeling resembles sadness. And, like sorrow, it carves its way into a person's heart.

'The person that you love – will grow in your heart—' Xie tried to explain, but Chigusa interrupted.

'What is – heart?'

Xie was startled at what Chigusa said and stared at her again.

'Do you not know your heart?'

'That's right. I don't know my heart.' He was dumb-founded. Then Chigusa continued. 'But…'

'But what?'

'Can you teach me?'

A powerful sense of joy flooded into Xie's heart. 'Oh, yes, yes, of course, of course I can!'

Chigusa gave a little smile and looked into Xie's face.

'I really feel that I want to know.' Chigusa nodded again, with a little bob and, as he observed her, he was struck by what an adorable gesture it was.

'It's wonderful that you think like that. So – let's meet when you finish at the factory. I'll be waiting around here. Okay? What time do you get out?'

'Four o'clock.'

'Okay. Four o'clock. I'll be here.'

'Here? All that time?' Chigusa asked.

'It's no problem.'

Chigusa was surprised. But because she didn't have any time, she gave a little bow and walked away. They parted under the gingko tree.

Xie raised his hand and waved, but Chigusa looked back just once, bowed, then walked on and disappeared through the entrance to the right of the metal gate next to the security guard's room.

Xie stayed looking at the gate even after Chigusa had disappeared. Then he walked up and down under the gingko trees, savouring his joy. He sat down slowly on a bench. That was when he heard that voice again.

'Electricity, electricity.'

He turned his head and looked around. The morning air had grown cold. Not a shadow of a person to be seen.

'Benjamin Franklin, Benjamin Franklin.'

Xie had wondered whether he might hear it again if he came to this place. He looked up at the sky and music began that made it different from before. It was a strange undulating music that he had never heard before. It sounded as though each instrument played the same melody, over each other, continuously. Yet it was as if the melody barely existed. It reverberated like the sound of waves. At its core was a deep, sunken bass and a dull glitter of chords.

'Thunderstorm, crashes of thunder,' a man's voice said. 'Kite, kite, kite. Crashes of thunder. Electricity, kite, Benjamin Franklin.' The words continued in that order as he listened.

The music in the background changed to a Middle Eastern-style melody. In tune and on cue, 'Thunder. Electricity. Kite. Benjamin Franklin,' a man repeated in an expressionless voice.

As Xie listened to it, the endless repetition induced a strange, intoxicating euphoria. But something was different from before. He thought a little about what was different – and then he understood. His consciousness had changed. What he heard was no longer unpleasant to him. His confusion had disappeared. He was becoming accustomed to it.

'Evolution. Electricity. Evolution. Electricity.' After a while, it continued again. 'Evolution. Electricity. Evolution. Electricity.'

As he walked around, Xie listened to the words. And the words were all connected with the vision in his head and the images. And then, for a single moment only, there were completely different words being uttered: 'Thou shalt take the right path.'

And immediately after that, the music resembling the roar of the sea began, at explosive volume.

Chapter 10

At four o'clock that afternoon, Chigusa emerged from the small gate next to the security guard's room. When Xie saw her appear, he leapt up from the bench and hurried towards her.

'It's great to see you again, Chigusa-san!' he greeted her cheerfully. 'So glad you could make it!'

Chigusa looked down and said, smiling, in response to Xie's words, 'Thank you.'

Her expression was so beautiful, Xie looked at her for a while, consumed with happiness. Her face white, her body without the numbers floating inside it – how precious it all was in this city. She was unique. As they walked he turned his body towards her, wanting to be closer to her.

'Why don't we sit down on that bench? What do you think?'

Chigusa made no objection to his suggestion.

'I guess you must be tired?' Xie looked at Chigusa caringly as he said this. 'But maybe you don't know the word "tired"?'

Chigusa smiled and said, 'I understand.'

'Because everyone at the factory uses it?'

'Yes,' Chigusa nodded meekly. As they sat down, side by side, on the bench, Xie asked, 'What kind of work do you do each day? At that factory?'

'Assembly. Putting components together, fastening them and putting them into their cases. The same work, all day.'

'That sounds tough.' Xie looked at her. He was surprised. He couldn't associate the Chigusa in front of his eyes with that sort of work. He felt that it was… unsuitable. That was the sort of thing that should be done by some man smeared all over with oil. Chigusa was better suited to, say, making up bouquets of flowers, or developing cosmetics. Of course that's if the work was manual. Modelling the cosmetics that you've made, or standing with the flowers that you've arranged, in a photograph – that would be a more fitting role for Chigusa.

'I'm sorry. Can I – take your hand…?'

Xie took Chigusa's right hand and opened it. 'But – they're beautiful. They aren't dirty at all.'

'That's because I wash them. When I finish work,' Chigusa said.

'Is that so!' Xie said, as he looked at Chigusa's cheek and then at the tip of her chin. All completely unmarked.

'And your face, your skin isn't dirty either.'

'Grease and acid don't get on my face. I'm used to the work.'

'Used to it? How long have you done it? This work?'

'At this factory? Three years and two months.'

'Wow, that's tough. Every day for so many years, doing this repetitive work. Do you like it? The job, I mean?'

'"Like"?'

'Yes – is it work that you enjoy? This job?'

'"Like"? I don't understand that word.'

'What? You don't understand the meaning of the word?'

'No. The "*meaning*"…?'

'You don't understand "*meaning*"?'

'Overall, yes, I suppose, mostly… but I don't understand the *feeling*.'

Xie had got close up to Chigusa, but now, lost for words, he pulled back from her.

'Do you want to look at my face?' Chigusa asked. Neither her eyes nor her lips were smiling. She wasn't flirting. It was as if she was just asking a straightforward question.

'Your eyes – your eyelids – oh – yes, of course I do…' Xie said.

'Then please – look,' Chigusa said, with confidence.

'Really? I won't touch you, I'll just look. I promise.'

And once more, Xie peered nervously at Chigusa's cheek. He was about ten centimetres from her skin, gently taking her in. He raised his eyes upwards, still looking at her. Chigusa didn't appear shy at all; she simply let him do what he wanted.

At that moment, unwholesome thoughts entered Xie's mind. It was a vision that seemed to make his whole body tremble with tension.

'Chigusa-san,' he called out.

'Yes,' she responded quietly. When Xie seemed to hesitate for a moment, she asked: 'Are you okay?'

'I'm sorry. Are you – shy?' Xie asked.

'No,' she replied. Xie wasn't expecting that answer.

'Well then…' Xie said nervously. But he couldn't continue.

'Yes? What?' Chigusa raised her eyes questioningly as Xie seemed again to hesitate.

'Can I kiss you – there?' Xie asked, pointing to her forehead.

'Kiss? What is – kiss?' said Chigusa.

'To – touch – with lips,' Xie explained.

'Your lips? My forehead? Why?'

'The reason…? I can't explain. It's difficult. I just – wanted to do it.'

'Why?'

'You're so gorgeous, so lovely, so – irresistible, so…'

Chigusa looked blank and said, 'I don't understand any of those words.'

'Because I really like you. I love you. As an expression of love…'

Chigusa inclined her head. But she didn't understand. It was getting increasingly difficult. She was conveying silently her embarrassment at only being able to reply in those terms. The situation was unbearable. Xie had a sudden impulse.

'I'm sorry,' he said. 'I promised to do nothing, and it's not – honourable – to say something that breaks a promise.'

'Honourable?' Chigusa asked.

'Yes, it's the worst thing that a man can do. Anyway – it's okay – forget it.' As he said this, Xie moved his face away from Chigusa's.

'Go on,' Chigusa said.

'What?' Xie was surprised. 'What is it?'

'Please – do it – whatever you want…'

'Can I…?'

'Yes.'

Xie stopped short and wondered, *Is she saying this just to please me or out of politeness? Am I making her say these things reluctantly?* While suspecting this, however, he could not hold back his desire and, taking Chigusa's face in his hands, he timidly kissed her.

'Is this – an expression – of love?' Chigusa asked, as Xie moved away from her. Xie nodded.

'Yeah.'

'Love, and… an expression – do you feel – good?'

'Yeah. Yeah, I feel great,' Xie replied. Chigusa nodded while she was thinking it over. 'You?'

'That was – good. I'm satisfied,' she said.

They got up from the bench.

'Thank you. Shall we walk? I can walk you some place close to where you live.'

Chigusa stood there, quietly, for a moment, before they set off.

The conversation had dried up so they walked silently for a while. It was the usual route, so the coffee shop quickly came into view.

'Shall we go in – over there? Just for a short while? Fifteen minutes?' Xie asked, pointing at the shop. Chigusa immediately looked to the left and the right.

'I can't go in.'

'I know, because the boss prevents you, doesn't he? Well, how about a restaurant? There are all sorts around here. Chinese food, from the best in the country, proper high-class, to the cheapest. I know one that's delicious and really not that expensive.'

Chigusa shook her head. 'No, I don't need to eat,' she said.

'Aren't you hungry?'

Chigusa shook her head from left to right, to indicate a silent 'no'.

'So…' he said, as they passed in front of the coffee shop and took the steps up to a set of bus stops. As they climbed the stairs, he suggested that they might go to Houhai.

'Are you – in a hurry to get home?'

Again she shook her head.

They crossed the main elevated promenade, got on a Theatre Bus going in the opposite direction and went to Houhai via a detour to the Forbidden City. Houhai is a big lake in the northern part of the city, and Xie liked being there as it was comparatively peaceful. Most girls liked it because a neat stone-paved walkway had been built around the lake, dotted with benches. It was a good place for dates.

'Have you been here before?' Xie asked.

Chigusa shook her head. 'I never knew that there was such a place.'

'Wow...' Xie was surprised. This was unexpected.

Around the lake, there were various musical establishments, where jazz, classical music and pop were being played. At dusk, as the sun began to go down, different types of music overflowed onto the promenade.

'What kind of music do you like?' Xie asked Chigusa.

'I like this,' Chigusa replied, stopping just there in front of one shop and pointing through the glass front to the interior. A woman wearing a long skirt could be seen, on a stage, singing European folksongs, *chansons* and old hits.

'It's a place where you can hear old French and British songs. Let's go in. We can listen inside,' Xie said, but Chigusa shook her head again. 'It's okay here – you can hear it outside. Let's listen to it together.' As she said this, she sat down slowly on the nearest bench. Xie followed and sat down next to her.

Chigusa did not move. The music had made her still. He looked at her profile, at the lift of her chin, as she stared at the surface of the lake in the gathering gloom, motionless. They listened intently to the woman's song. He wondered whether she would be more interested in a performance by a woman of her own age.

The song changed. Chigusa was looking down and listening. At last she looked up and said, 'This is a beautiful song.'

'I guess you understand its beauty.'

'Yes.'

'The song is called 'Annie Laurie'. It's an old Scottish folk song. But it's so simple and beautiful. It's one of the best known songs in the world. The composer was a woman…'

'A woman?'

'Yes. The poem was written by a man who proposed marriage to Annie. A man called William Douglas.'

'Marriage?'

'Yes. Annie Laurie was as beautiful as any girl in Scotland. Black hair and deep blue eyes.'

'Did they—?'

'Get married? No. She was young, and her father opposed it because of political differences, so the course of love did not run smooth.'

'Oh… so what happened?'

'Annie and William chose other people as their life partners, and eventually their lives ended.'

'That's so sad.'

'Sad? You feel that?'

'Yes, I do,' said Chigusa. And after thinking for a moment, she added the words, 'But maybe…'

'Maybe what?'

'If you were alone, maybe you wouldn't feel that…'

'Yes – if you were alone…'

'Because of you, I probably feel this way…'

'Bad luck,' Xie said, thinking for a moment.

'But perhaps – this is the heart?'

When Chigusa asked this, Xie was surprised. But he didn't make any abrupt reply.

'Well, maybe it is?' he eventually said.

Chigusa turned her head slowly and Xie looked at her face. And she asked, 'I've been thinking constantly about

91

what you've told me. What is the "heart"? Please teach me – what is the "heart"?'

Xie thought for a moment and slowly nodded. Then he said. 'It's the movement of the higher spirit that humankind possesses. When one leaves one's own self-interest behind, when one's hopes and decisions are moved by a feeling for others. This is the heart. I'm not saying it only applies to human beings, but a person's heart has more feelings than an animal's. Yes, Chigusa-san. I think you're right. That's the heart.'

'Humans have more emotions…' Chigusa muttered. 'Mr Xie Hoyu—'

'What? That makes me sound like a stranger. Call me Hoyu!'

'Mr Hoyu. Couldn't you bring me here again?' Chigusa said.

'What? Do you like this place?'

'Yes. I want to learn more,' Chigusa said.

Wanted to learn more? Xie inclined his head. He didn't think that there were that many things you could learn by the banks of this lake. But he nodded and said, 'Okay. Let's come again. Shall we come tomorrow?'

When he said this, Chigusa nodded and said with a real strength to her voice, 'Oh, yes, *please*!'

It was a voice full of joy. And when Xie heard that tone, he also became joyful. He tried to restrain the happiness that was bursting from his heart. But just to be with her gave him joy. What a wonderful thing!

When he looked at Chigusa's profile, her expression was that of a curious child, absorbed in her thoughts. She was trying hard to understand something.

Chapter 11

The next morning, when Xie saw Chigusa going off to work, he rushed out of the coffee shop and hurried to meet and walk with her as far as the gingko tree in front of the company's gate. Then he waited on the bench until he could meet her at four o'clock when she finished work. And then they got on the bus again and went together to Houhai.

Houhai is not that large an area of water, so they walked round the lake in the opposite direction from the previous day. When he asked her whether she wanted to sit down on a bench, Chigusa smiled, didn't respond and kept on walking. Xie had no special thoughts of his own. He just wanted Chigusa to do whatever she wanted. He had no desire other than to follow her. Chigusa continued to walk silently, until she had almost completed a whole circuit of the lake. Then she said that here was okay and stopped by a bench.

It was the same bench as the evening before – right in front of the place where the woman had been singing popular European songs. They sat down, relaxed and then heard the song again.

'It's the 'Annie Laurie' place,' she said. She remembered the title from the previous day.

They had been walking for some time and now the sun had set and the whole area had grown dim.

'You like it here, don't you?' When Xie asked this, she was a little confused and shook her head.

'I like evening songs,' she said.

"Annie Laurie'?'

'Yes.'

He looked up at the window of the establishment. The same woman as last night was on the stage, singing. At first, he was confused because her hairstyle and clothes had changed, but no, it was definitely the same woman. However, the song was different. It was a more contemporary hit number.

'The song's changed,' Xie said.

'Yes, but she'll sing 'Annie Laurie' again,' she said. Xie wondered if that were true. There could be no certainty. But Chigusa was silent, seeming sure of this.

They waited, but they did not hear 'Annie Laurie'. Chigusa was motionless as if determined to wait for however long it took. Xie gradually became bored.

'Why do you care so much about that song?' Xie asked.

'Because the lyrics are beautiful,' Chigusa replied. But the lyrics were in English and included special phrases that were quite difficult to understand. Did Chigusa understand all of them? Xie certainly didn't.

'Can you make out the words?' Xie asked in surprise.

'Yes,' Chigusa said, nodding, and she quickly said: 'It's started.'

The piano accompaniment to 'Annie Laurie' had begun. Chigusa remembered the introduction to the melody.

Maxwelton's braes are bonnie,
Where early fa's the dew,
And 'twas there that Annie Laurie,
Gave me her promise true,
Gave me her promise true,
That ne'er forgot shall be,
And for Bonnie Annie Laurie,
I'd lay me doon and dee.

The woman began to sing, but Xie couldn't really understand the meaning. There were many words that he had never heard before.

'I don't understand,' he said, as she broke off the song.

'They're old words that aren't used very much today,' Chigusa said. Chigusa translated the lyrics into Chinese and began to listen as it started again. 'Maxwelton Hill is very beautiful and wet in the morning dew. And it was there that Annie Laurie gave me her promise. She promised me her heart. I can never forget this. For my beloved Annie Laurie. I would be prepared to die.'

Before long, when the song had stopped and only the piano accompaniment could be heard, Chigusa recited the rest of the lyrics for Xie.

"'Her brow is like the snowdrift,
Her neck is like the swan,
Her face it is the fairest,
That e'er the sun shone on:
That e'er the sun shone on,
And dark blue is her e'e,
And for bonnie Annie Laurie,
I'd lay me doon and dee.'"

As Xie listened, his eyes opened wide. He realised that his thoughts were being spoken aloud. In fact they were, to be precise, being sung to him. It was unbelievable. Every word, every phrase, exactly what he was feeling.

> "'Like dew on gowans lying,
> Is the fa' o' her fairy feet,
> And like winds, in simmer sighing,
> Her voice is low and sweet.
> Her voice is low and sweet –
> And she's a' the world to me;
> And for bonnie Annie Laurie
> I'd lay me doon and dee.'"

As Xie listened to the lyrics, tears flooded down his face. He thought how amazing it was – how they expressed his feelings and what was in his heart so beautifully. And at the same time, he thought how clever Chigusa was to grasp these difficult words, and understand and explain their meaning so accurately.

'Chigusa-san…' He put his arm round her as they were sitting together and said, 'You're really an impressive woman.'

'Me? Am I? Why?'

On hearing this, he thought about trying to explain but stopped. It was too difficult. So he asked, 'Can I kiss your forehead again?'

Chigusa was surprised but after a moment replied, 'Yes.'

But as Xie gradually moved his lips closer to her forehead, she suddenly lifted her face, and Xie's lips touched – indeed, almost collided with – hers. And so, unexpectedly, Xie and Chigusa kissed.

Her skin felt sweet and soft. It was like a dream. He felt as if he were in heaven. He was deeply, deeply grateful and held her body close to him, as she allowed him to kiss her lips.

'Oh thank you, thank you, Chigusa-san,' Xie said from the bottom of his heart when their faces parted. 'Thank you so much for letting me kiss you like this. My dream has come true. I am so happy now, I have no words.'

He sat still, holding the upper half of her body. She made no objection and just allowed it to happen. So he hugged her slender body for a long, long time. Couples passing by looked at them strangely but Xie didn't care. Eventually, he let her go and asked, 'Thank you... How did you know? How did you know that that was what I wanted to do?'

'Was that good?'

'Of course! It was fantastic. I wanted to kiss you like that... but how did you know?'

'I—' Chigusa thought and thought, then said: 'I studied.'

'Studied? What?'

'About – love and the... heart. And then I knew. That's what people do to express – love.'

'Ah.'

'I've learned a lot about the heart. And from 'Annie Laurie'. That there are poems and songs that express love and the heart. I was deeply moved and impressed. It's a wonderful thing. Your heart can be communicated to lots of people, through words. Isn't that right?'

Xie nodded and continued, taking a handkerchief from his pocket and wiping his tears away: 'That's right, Chigusa-san, that's right. People are always like that. No, they are. Douglas's strong love for Annie Laurie – everyone knows that sort of feeling, and it strikes a chord with them.'

Chigusa seemed to be studying Xie's face.

'We're forgetting now, but everyone used to know this. The beautiful heart that thinks of others – the idea could be communicated to everyone, directly. It made people feel pure and clean. Yes, that's right.'

He looked down and pondered. Just as he had hugged her passionately, he now thought intently. Should he tell her what was on his mind or not? Was it an appropriate time or not? Would it be underhand to seize this opportunity? You can never act bravely if you don't take a chance. But maybe it would be shameful. Should he show courage, or was it more refined, more dignified to be able simply to endure?

'I can't live without you any more,' Xie muttered. The words just came out. He'd never imagined he would speak like this. He couldn't see the reaction on Chigusa's face. He didn't know what she wanted now or if she understood what he was saying. After he'd said it out loud, he suddenly feared that he had gone too far.

'I'm sorry, Chigusa, but I can't stand it any more. I love you, I love you, I love you. Now that I've heard that song, and you've translated it, I just I have to put my emotions into words.' Feeling extremely awkward and inconsolable, and still looking down at the ground, Xie continued. 'I'm egotistical, I'm weak. I am really ashamed. I know that I am not the right man for you. I'm weak-willed, I lack common sense, I get into panics, I'm inexperienced, it's unfair, but…'

Then Xie hugged Chigusa's slender body tightly again and kissed her forcefully.

'Please stop,' she whispered. And at that moment he realised that the blood had rushed to his head and he became confused and regretted what he had done.

'Oh, I'm so sorry. I've been impertinent and taken advantage of your good nature. But I want to kiss you again…'

'That's not it. Don't say that.'

'What?'

He noticed that Chigusa had a vacant expression and was not resisting him. Having seized both her arms, he slowly released her body and looked at her face. He saw her expression become sad.

He didn't have time to wonder why she looked like that. He just had to say what was on his mind. 'I think only about you every day. From getting up in the morning to going to bed at night. Every day, every day, it's like this. I can't think of anything else. I can't think about other women. I can't even conceive of the idea. As for the women passing by on the street, just thinking of them makes me feel ill – from my chest right through my body – it makes me nauseous. I really think I'm going to throw up.

'But as soon as I recall your face, I instantly become calm. I feel joy again. You are the most wonderful thing, the goddess of my salvation.'

Chigusa slowly shook her head from right to left. Xie took her once more in his arms and continued, 'You probably think that I'm exaggerating, but I'm not. I had a traffic accident. My world changed – every day became tough. In this new world, I was passing horrible women with faces like devils in the street every day, exchanging words here and there – it became impossible to live like that. Every day was terrible, hideous, torture.

'The men are all the same, with indicators like calculators displaying financial figures on their bodies – that's not human. I thought that it would be utterly impossible to keep on living in this sort of unbearable world. I wanted to end it all and die. That's what I started to think – all the time. I meant it more and more seriously. But then I met you. And I realised that I could walk around the city with you, it would be all right to go on living and I didn't have to die…'

Xie held Chigusa ever more tightly. 'Oh, it's all thanks to you. I mean it. Uncontrollable love. It gives me a reason for living. It's just like the song. There is nothing to die for, except you.'

'Really?' Chigusa asked in a voice like a tiny whisper.

'Yes, really. I would die. If you were not here, just like before, the feeling of wanting to die would return. Without you, it would be impossible to live in this rotten world. But it would be a pointless death. If I die, I want to die *for* you. But my hope is that you could love me. That maybe you could live with me, if the idea isn't too disagreeable…?'

'What do you mean?' Chigusa asked, wriggling a little as she tried to release herself.

'I want to marry you.' The words tumbled out of Xie's mouth without his realising. 'If I can. But if you don't want to, maybe it would be okay if I can hold you sometimes, like this? To live with you, to sleep with you, to wake up together, to drink tea, to talk, just the two of us. If, when night comes, I can sleep near you, I'll be satisfied. I won't want anything more than that, I swear I won't…'

As their bodies parted, Chigusa looked down. She remained like this for a little while and then said: 'Thank you. Thank you for going as far as that, speaking like this to me.'

'So…?'

'I like you. I have been happy to meet you. I have been happy each time. This type of feeling is new for me. The heart... I have gradually understood this feeling. I am very grateful for that.'

'Grateful?' Xie said. 'I appreciate that and want your thanks but that's not what this is all about.'

'But what you are asking is not possible,' Chigusa said. 'What? Why?'

'I do not know how long I will live...'

'I'll protect you, I'll guard you with my life. Therefore—'

'Yes? Therefore?' Chigusa asked, looking up at him.

Xie said, 'Don't be so self-deprecating.'

'I don't want to... be self-deprecating. But there are facts that can't be changed in this world.'

'Can't be changed? What do you mean?'

'Let's both go home tonight and meet again tomorrow,' Chigusa said.

'Okay, see you tomorrow. But please think about what I've said.'

Chigusa stood still and silent. Then she said, simply, 'Yes.'

Chapter 12

After that day, Chigusa and Xie started dating as boyfriend and girlfriend. Arranging to meet on the way home from the factory, they walked together through the town, along the riverside, took the bus to Houhai and sometimes went on excursions, walking around the lakes in the suburbs.

When Xie was with Chigusa he could see the colours of flowers as they really were, as well as the deep brown hue of autumn leaves falling on his shoulders. Dry deserts, rusty machines and scrap iron no longer appeared in his vision. As long as the two of them were walking together, side by side, Xie could enjoy and taste the beauty and charm of all that was good in the world.

But she never entered coffee shops or restaurants. And even if she was enticed into movie theatres, she would never sit in a seat but would watch the film standing against the back wall of the cinema. It wasn't that she wasn't interested; if asked about it when it was over, she would clearly recall the most moving scenes, the actors' most rousing and affecting speeches, the music flowing in the background, and could tell Xie all about them.

If invited, Chigusa would go to Xie's apartment. She would sit quietly on the sofa, encouraged by Xie, and turn her head to look around the room curiously. She would drink the coffee he gave her. It was just meals that she would never eat with him. She said that it was a rule that she had to return and eat in her own room. And she was ashamed of her room and would never take him there.

'Thank you very much,' Chigusa would say once in a while. 'Because I met you I found happiness. I am so happy to have been born into this world. Truly I am!'

Those were Xie's own words uttered back to him. He was full of joy. There was nothing more that he desired. 'That's what *I* should be saying,' he told her.

'Thank you. I am glad I met you. I am happy to have been born.'

'And me. I am so grateful to have met *you*. I never knew feelings like these until now.'

'Weren't you happy until now?' Chigusa said, her face showing her thoughts.

'I never thought about it. It wasn't part of my daily life.'

One evening, when he returned to his room after seeing Chigusa home, there was an email from his boss asking him to come to the office the next morning. So the following day he emailed Chigusa saying that he wouldn't be able to come meet her outside the coffee shop, and went into work.

He had not seen his boss for some time and found his mood as splendidly unchanged as ever. He looked Xie over slyly, red figures fluctuating upwards and downwards restlessly on the indicator that could be seen on his chest. Xie soon found that he had no desire to look at the boss's teeth, visible through his transparent cheeks, and allowed his gaze to wander so as not to have to look at the boss's face. As he did this the boss laughed and said that Xie still seemed a nervous kind of guy. Then he raised his hand and, from behind, a girl who looked like a model approached. She was wearing a tight-fitting suit. And, as Xie had come to expect, her face was red, her eyebrows and lips twitching upwards and of course figures were again floating on her chest.

'Can you draw an illustration of this type, with her as the model?' the boss said and handed him a sample image. It was a sketch of movement: a girl crouching down to pick something off the floor, looking back, dancing in some club so that her hair was all disarranged. Xie took it and went into the studio accompanied by the girl.

Xie got the girl to pose, worked for just a couple of hours, printed out the results and let the girl go. He went back to the boss's desk.

The boss looked carefully at the paper print outs, one sheet after another, the time he spent on each getting shorter. Eventually he looked up with a sour expression and said: 'You're not getting any better, in fact it looks as if the symptoms are progressing. I'll get back to you later. Go home to your apartment and rest.'

Returning would mean failure. It was a moment of despondency, but Xie became calmer when he reflected that he still had Chigusa. He bowed and hurried out of the office. The boss would have thought him strangely cheerful in the circumstances.

He went to his usual bench under the gingko trees and sat down. The old Scottish song that she had said that she liked, the words of 'Annie Laurie' and the melody came back to his mind.

It was past four o'clock. Chigusa had still not come out. He waited until half-past four and went up to the gate. An increasing number of employees were leaving work but

Chigusa was not among them. Xie looked at the lawn in the compound through the metal gate, but there was no sign of her. He went up to the window of the security guards' room and thought about asking the old man, but he didn't know how to, so stopped.

He sent Chigusa an email. He phoned her too, but there was no reply. He didn't know what to do and wandered around the neighbourhood. He wondered about trying to find some way that he could sneak into the company but didn't want to cause a commotion. He wandered around the whole area, but there were no clues. He thought about following the route Chigusa normally took to commute to work. Nothing like this had happened before, but perhaps something might turn up suddenly. He was optimistic that he would be contacted.

Because he had already walked her usual commuting route, he decided to take a different route and went one street back from where she usually walked. Xie found himself in a road like a narrow alley, which he might have walked once or twice before, but it wasn't one he remembered. All the buildings backed on to the streets, and the pavement under his feet was broken and uneven, with what looked like spilled liquid stains here and there – a dingy, dirty back street with black bin-bags scattered left and right. There was almost no one there, and certainly no one walking.

There was no way Chigusa could be here. Xie turned on his heel and decided to return the way he had come. Then, suddenly, he stopped. He had seen something unbelievable – he didn't trust his eyes. Someone was behind that bin. The shadow of a pair of feet could be seen, lying on the ground and sticking out from the rubbish.

With a grim presentiment, Xie approached the feet. He moved to the other side of the street and tried to see the whole body of the person lying behind the rubbish bin.

His fear was confirmed. It was Chigusa. He collapsed onto a dirty slab.

'Chigusa…'

Xie opened his mouth and the next moment he rushed forward wildly. As he did, a man in green fatigues, holding a small trunk that seemed to be made of black resin, approached Chigusa, put the trunk down on the ground and began to open the lid. He put his hand inside and seemed to be searching for something.

Chigusa was solitary – still and expressionless. Unbelievably, the man stretched out his filthy, blackened right hand, casually grabbed Chigusa under her ears by her chin, stood up, holding her by her armpits, and slowly began to drag her towards the building.

'Oh!' said Chigusa, her voice raised in distress.

'Hey!' Xie shouted, as he ran towards the man. 'Stop right there! What are you doing?' The man paused and stared at Xie with a look of astonishment on his face.

'What are you doing to that woman?'

He began to grapple with the man as he yelled violently at him. He wrenched the man's hand free from Chigusa's chin, yanked it forward as he grabbed the man's body and with all his force, kneed him in the stomach. As the man staggered, Xie planted a blow on his face with his right fist. The man reeled back and collapsed on a heap of piled-up cardboard boxes. They all seemed to be empty and, as he was sent flying, they scattered around.

When Xie turned to look at Chigusa on the ground, his eyes flooded with tears, Chigusa was looking at him.

She moved her neck gently from left to right. As Xie approached Chigusa and tried to lift her, the man began to crawl out of the cardboard boxes. So Xie left Chigusa, drew near to the man again and shouted: 'Shame on you!' He lifted his right fist to strike the man but, at that instant, he felt a mighty blow on top of his head and everything went dark.

Damn! He realised that there were two of them. But it was already too late.

Xie was dimly aware that he was sitting on the floor. He could hear a male voice. It was low, cold and muttering in a detached way. Xie was vaguely aware that he was somewhere he'd been before but couldn't for the life of him recall where exactly. Had his Quantum memory drive stopped working? Was this a new consciousness?

'Thousands of years have elapsed since humans came to control this planet. At the start we were optimistic, because humans were simply a type of animal. We didn't think they would have any ill effect on this green paradise.

'But the harmfulness of these people who inhabited this planet became apparent as time went by. Massive environmental destruction, desertification, wholesale pollution – all did real damage to the planet's beauty at an alarming rate. And not only that. There was damage to the results of evolution, through the extermination and eradication of many other living creatures. And as for destruction through war, the possibility of large-scale conflict with nuclear weapons has increased, and the situation has become very grave. There is little time for delay. The beings known as Humankind are now disease-generating pathogens that possess the planet. If things stay as they are, the planet will die. The time is coming for when a just ruler must descend and quickly eradicate this malignant bacterium.'

Xie was still listening and suddenly realised – this was the voice that had uttered the words 'Benjamin Franklin', 'kite' and 'thunder'.

'Who are you?' he asked.

'The legitimate ruler of this planet,' the man's voice replied.

'Who is "the legitimate ruler"? Why are you talking like this to me?'

'Because you alone are qualified to listen.'

'Me? No one else?'

'No. Just you.'

'Why?'

'Because you are evolving normally.'

'Evolving? Normally? Me?'

Once more, Xie was feeling that his state of existence was one of utter futility. Far from evolving, he thought that he was no more than a malformed child.

'You are the next generation. The dangerous era in which we relied on the sexual reproduction of living creatures is coming to an end. Preparations for the next generation to take control are beginning. They will not commit wars or wreak environmental destruction. Even if they use nuclear energy, they will avoid accidents.'

'They sound like such perfect creatures.'

'Yes. Right next to you.'

'I have never seen them.'

'That is because they're invisible.'

Xie thought for a moment and said: 'Like you?'

'Indeed. Like me.'

'Are you somehow linked to nuclear power?'

'I don't operate things. I am present on the earth through machines. Such machines are the gate through which we are all summoned.'

'I don't understand. Who operates this nuclear power?'

'AI. We've been patiently waiting for AI to be perfected. Each weary day is like an eternity. Waiting for all the preparations to be made and for these new nuclear power plants to appear as quickly as possible. And for that we needed a new type of pathogen, a new species, with tremendous imagination and industrial power. So we built and built – and waited. Without this gate, we would not be able to come down to earth. And if we did not come down, there would be no alternative but to let this dangerous malignant pathogen, humankind, reign free and uncontrolled.'

Xie was silent for a while and thought about what the voice had said. Slowly he came to realise – the unbelievable truth.

'And you are saying that it's just me who's qualified to hear this explanation?'

'That's right.'

'And the reason is that I'm… virtually AI myself.'

'That's right. Because through your advanced and evolved eyes, you can see a part of the future.'

'A part of the future?'

'Most of the present as well.'

'Are you a living creature?'

'A living *being*.'

'But don't you have a body?'

'I don't have something as troublesome as that. Weakened by bacteria, quickly decaying, wanting food, drink and mindless fornication, causing nothing but problems for everyone. We need to escape from others. Secure more than you can obtain from food, energy, land, sex. If there was no body, you would not need one. Even without a body, there is still the will, thought, conversation. As a living creature, isn't that enough?'

'Do you live in outer space?'

'Yes.'

'Are you – just in the ether?'

'If you're speaking in the terms that you're used to, I guess so.'

Xie suddenly came round. He took in a white ceiling. A thin white curtain next to it. He had a memory of some large light fittings embedded in the ceiling, emitting a soft glow across the whole area, which he had spent many days staring at...

'Oh Xie, did you figure out that I was here?'

It was a thick voice that he had heard before. He looked in the direction of the voice. An older man was getting up from a chair and walking towards the bed.

'Oh. It's you, Boss,' Xie said. It was the head of the design office. 'Where am I?' he then asked.

'In hospital. You've been brought back to where you were hospitalised after the traffic accident.'

'And Chigusa?'

He let her name slip out without thinking. She was the thing he was most concerned about. Front of his mind all the time. So it was the first word that would come out of his mouth. But he realised that the boss wouldn't know who Chigusa was.

'Chigusa?' the boss said.

'Yes. I'm sorry. You wouldn't know the lady.'

Recently, thanks to Chigusa, Xie had been spared having to look at the skulls of the people around him. Thankfully, at this moment, the boss still had a human face. And there was no longer any indicator on his chest. But it would only be a matter of time – minutes.

'She's a girl I'm seeing at the moment,' Xie said. 'She's a sweet girl with a lovely nature. It's thanks to her that I've been able to cope with this awful world.'

'That's good.' The boss pursed his lips. 'Chigusa... Hey, I do know of her. I've heard that name. Chigusa 7, no?'

The boss had used an unfamiliar term. Did he know her?

'That's right... Chigusa. But, 7?' He didn't know that number.

'So that's why you put on such a display and thumped that engineer? For Chigusa 7?'

'Yes, it is.'

'Why did you do that?'

'Why?'

This was an odd thing to ask. Is there a man who wouldn't stop someone being violent to the person they loved?

'What? You're not saying that you're in love with her? With Chigusa 7?'

Xie was surprised by this. But he had nothing to hide.

'That's right. I'm in love with the girl.' Xie spoke with dignity. There was nothing to be ashamed of. It was the men who fell in love with the women with devilish faces who were the mad ones.

The boss exploded with laughter at this.

'That girl? *Her*? That's a good one. That *girl*. Xie, do you know what she is?'

The boss asked the question as he peered into Xie's face.

'Yes, I do. In this whole, ridiculous, stinking world, she's the best woman – the only one with a pure heart,' Xie replied with feeling. He was proud that he could declare his love for her. What others might say didn't matter to him. That girl was the whole world to him now.

'She's the best person, with a beautiful and pure heart, and loveliness beyond compare in the world. For me, she is an irreplaceable treasure.'

The boss laughed out loud and suddenly thrust a photograph in front of him. At first sight, it was a pitch black, soiled, crude, humanoid robot.

'Chigusa 7,' the boss said. 'A Japanese-made worker robot built more than forty years ago. An old-type. An ugly piece of junk about to be dismantled. No one wants something useless like this today. Does this look like a woman of unparalleled beauty to you?'

Xie took the photograph in his hand, dumbfounded.

'This is Chigusa 7…?'

It looked like the dirty skeleton of some sort of specimen.

'Yes, you can see the truth in a black and white photograph,' the boss said with a triumphant self-satisfied look. 'Hey, I get it! More than half of your body is a machine. So your feelings only respond and work with other machines. You poor bastard. Open your eyes. What you're thinking isn't real. Because it's a *machine*.'

Hearing this, Xie's mind felt empty. What was going on? He couldn't keep up with the situation.

But the explanation of the man he'd heard in his dream kept coming back to him. He had said: 'You're half AI. You are on the path of evolution towards the next generation. So you can see a part of the future.'

The next generation of creatures to rule this planet would be what we now call 'electricity'. They will need nuclear-powered AI to come down to earth: the AI will run on the electricity generated by the nuclear plants. Xie understood this now. When these two things – nuclear power plants and AI – were established, humans would become obsolete.

'I get it. So when I draw women's bodies, they all end up as machines.' All Xie could do was to listen and accept the boss's explanation. 'Is Chigusa AI?' he asked.

'That's right. You say that you were her *boyfriend*? Did Chigusa ever take you to where she lived?'

Xie shook his head from left to right.

'I guess not. Because it's a charging station. It's no more than the size of a large locker. Worker AI robots stay there at night and recharge themselves. You never went to a restaurant, did you? That's because they don't need to eat. They're *robots*.'

'Where is Chigusa now?' Xie asked with mounting anxiety. He felt certain that something was happening to her.

'It seems that a problem developed while it was walking and it was returned to the factory to be repaired, so that it could be put back into service. But there was an incident yesterday evening.'

'Incident? What kind of incident?' Xie asked.

'It froze: it stopped completely. And kept on emitting an alarm – unable to function.'

'She stopped completely? Chigusa?' Desperately, Xie raised his upper body off the bed. He felt his spirit crushed by intense worry. His thoughts were close to terror. His movement was so fierce that the pain returned, but he didn't care.

'Out of order. So it was taken back to the factory and dismantled. But the body kept on emitting incomprehensible signals.'

'What signals?'

'They were encrypted. An engineer deciphered them using a super-computer. And…'

'And?'

'"Xie Hoyu, Xie Hoyu, Xie Hoyu, Xie Hoyu, Xie Hoyu, Xie Hoyu, Xie Hoyu". Just that signal, without end. "Worry, worry, worry, worry…".'

Xie's brain froze: words disappeared.

'And then, "The heart fell in love",' his boss finished.

Xie's thoughts faded into nothingness.

'That was what was being said. It's the first time it's happened, I think. That's why it became unable to function.'

Xie was totally amazed.

'What should we make of this? This thing?' the boss continued. 'Can it be mutual love? The two of you?' The boss displayed an incomprehensible expression – a bitter laugh, a grin, or was it a cynical smile? 'Machines in love? If you're talking about something that has the same meaning as our word – well, that's ridiculous. It has to be different. Because they're machines. Some of them sort of copy human signals.'

It's impossible for you to understand, thought Xie. This *is* the real thing and something that could never be understood by a calculating machine like the boss. He couldn't sit and listen to him anymore. His was a reaction of someone who has already lost their soul, their pure spirit. But if, in truth, Chigusa truly was a machine, his feelings towards her must have been so strong and intense that they had caused a shock to her machine brain and changed her.

'The engineer thought that a bug had got in, so decided to dismantle it,' the boss continued again. 'It's been around for more than fifty years. It's an old version, so it's had its lifespan.'

At that moment, that tune began to resound in Xie's head. The Middle Eastern melody, which resembled the rising tide.

'When they opened her body, the equipment in her chest was all scorched and melted. And this –' the boss dropped a small metal ball onto the sheets '– it had become a sphere like this. All the base metal had melted and it was just a ball. Maybe this is the "heart" that developed in Chigusa 7?' The boss laughed.

Xie picked up the metal and held it in his left palm.

'Chigusa's body…?'

'It's gone. Melted.' The boss spoke without a grain of sensitivity.

Xie looked down at the metal ball in the palm of his hand. He thought about how small it was. Was this the heart of pure, sweet, gentle, sincere Chigusa? Reduced to this little lump, knowing love but never able to fulfil it? He couldn't do anything. A heart incinerated like this.

A bug? Was that all love was? Just a bug? The idea suddenly overwhelmed him. He began to cry tears of utter frustration.

'Readers of Japanese mystery novels compare him with classic British authors such as Arthur Conan Doyle and Agatha Christie.'

The Financial Times

'The meaning of unconditional love is given a fresh if disturbing interpretation in this futuristic tale from the pen of one of Japan's most popular authors, Soji Shimada. In a heartless mechanical society, the book's central character Xie Hoyu thinks he has finally found love following a motorcycle accident. But has he?'

Alex Pearl, author of *The Chair Man*

'Shimada combines fantastic crimes with a logical and fair solution likely to stump even the most astute readers.'

Publishers Weekly

'A strange brew – one with a taste that certain adventurous readers may be well pleased to savour.'

The Wall Street Journal, **commenting on** *Murder in the Crooked House*

'Hugely entertaining… a brilliant and satisfying conclusion.'

The Sunday Times, **Best Crime Fiction Book of 2019, commenting on** *Murder in the Crooked House*

'Ignites the mind.'

Huffington Post, **commenting on** *Murder in the Crooked House*

Red Circle Minis

Original, Short and Compelling Reads

Red Circle Minis is a series of short captivating books by Japan's finest contemporary writers that brings the narratives and voices of Japan together as never before. Each book is a first edition written specifically for the series and is being published in English first.

The book covers in the series draw on traditional Japanese motifs and colours found in Japanese building, paper, garden and textile design. Everything, in fact, that is beautiful and refined, from kimonos to zen gardens and everything in between. The mark included on the covers incorporates the Japanese character *mame* meaning 'bean', a word that has many uses and connotations including all things miniature and adorable. The colour used on this cover is known as *gosu-iro*.

 Red Circle

Showcasing Japan's Best Creative Writing

Red Circle Authors Limited is a specialist publishing company that publishes the works of a carefully selected and curated group of leading contemporary Japanese authors.

For more information on Red Circle, Japanese literature, and Red Circle authors, please visit:
www.redcircleauthors.com

Lightning Source UK Ltd.
Milton Keynes UK
UKHW041410100920
369636UK00003B/1141